IN HITLER'S BERLIN

the passion of an American millionaire for a beautiful and totally depraved titled Englishwoman gave birth to a monstrous new power in the world.

IN A LOCKED LONDON MANSION

a brilliant, tragically flawed man was kept prisoner for reasons only he and his captors knew.

IN THE SECRET COUNSELS OF THE KREMLIN

the strangest proposition of the twentieth century was pondered, one that would bring together communism and capitalism in an unholy alliance.

IN THE MIDNIGHT STREETS OF PARIS

a half-English, half-French intelligence agent found himself playing a lone hand in a last gamble against an unknown enemy who held all the high cards and whose killers were everywhere. . . .

THE DOUBLE-CROSS CIRCUIT

It will reach into your nightmares. . . .

"Deft . . . exciting spy-suspense thriller!"
—*Publishers Weekly*

Big Bestsellers from SIGNET

- ☐ LABYRINTH by Eric MacKenzie-Lamb. (#E9062—$2.25)*
- ☐ RITTER'S GOLD by Frank N. Hawkins, Jr. (#J9067—$1.95)*
- ☐ THE ENIGMA by Michael Barak. (#E8920—$1.95)*
- ☐ GOING ALL THE WAY by Susan Hufford. (#E9014—$2.25)*
- ☐ PACIFIC HOSPITAL by Robert H. Curtis. (#J9018—$1.95)*
- ☐ SAVAGE SNOW by Will Holt. (#E9019—$2.25)*
- ☐ CALENDAR OF SINNERS by Moira Lord. (#J9021—$1.95)*
- ☐ THE NIGHT LETTER by Paul Spike. (#E8947—$2.50)*
- ☐ FOOLS DIE by Mario Puzo. (#E8881—$3.50)
- ☐ THE GODFATHER by Mario Puzo. (#E8970—$2.75)
- ☐ THE MOSSAD by Dennis Eisenberg, Uri Dan and Eli Landau. (#E8883—$2.50)*
- ☐ PHOENIX by Amos Aricha and Eli Landau. (#E8692—$2.50)*
- ☐ EYE OF THE NEEDLE by Ken Follett. (#E8746—$2.95)
- ☐ YOUR CHEATIN' HEART by Elizabeth Gilchrist. (#E9061—$2.25)*
- ☐ THE SPEAR by James Herbert. (#E9060—$2.50)*

*Price slightly higher in Canada

Buy them at your local bookstore or use this convenient coupon for ordering.

THE NEW AMERICAN LIBRARY, INC.,
P.O. Box 999, Bergenfield, New Jersey 07621

Please send me the SIGNET BOOKS I have checked above. I am enclosing
$_____ (please add 50¢ to this order to cover postage and handling).
Send check or money order—no cash or C.O.D.'s. Prices and numbers are
subject to change without notice.

Name _____

Address _____

City_____ State_____ Zip Code_____

Allow 4-6 weeks for delivery.
This offer is subject to withdrawal without notice.

THE DOUBLE-CROSS CIRCUIT

A novel

by

Michael Dorland

A SIGNET BOOK
NEW AMERICAN LIBRARY
TIMES MIRROR

NAL BOOKS ARE ALSO AVAILABLE AT DISCOUNTS IN BULK QUANTITY FOR INDUSTRIAL OR SALES-PROMOTIONAL USE. FOR DETAILS, WRITE TO PREMIUM MARKETING DIVISION, NEW AMERICAN LIBRARY, INC., 1633 BROADWAY, NEW YORK, NEW YORK 10019.

COPYRIGHT © 1978 BY MICHAEL DORLAND

All rights reserved. No part of this book may be reproduced in any form or by any means, except for the inclusion of brief quotations in a review, without permission in writing from the publisher. For information address Grosset & Dunlap, Inc., 51 Madison Avenue, New York, New York 10010.

This is an authorized reprint of a hardcover edition published by Grosset & Dunlap, Inc.

 SIGNET TRADEMARK REG. U.S. PAT. OFF. AND FOREIGN COUNTRIES
REGISTERED TRADEMARK—MARCA REGISTRADA
HECHO EN CHICAGO, U.S.A.

SIGNET, SIGNET CLASSICS, MENTOR, PLUME AND MERIDIAN BOOKS
are published by The New American Library, Inc.,
1633 Broadway, New York, New York 10019

FIRST SIGNET PRINTING, FEBRUARY, 1980

1 2 3 4 5 6 7 8 9

PRINTED IN THE UNITED STATES OF AMERICA

For Anna and the Child

ACKNOWLEDGMENTS

Much of the factual material from which I have created GTT is inspired by the unsavory past of a real corporation. I would like, therefore, to acknowledge the debt owed to British journalist Anthony Sampson for his remarkable book, *The Sovereign State of ITT*.

Also, to David Kahn for his illuminating work on coding machines in *The Codebreakers*.

And, finally, to Yves Courrière for his monumental four-volume *La Guerre d'Algérie*.

What remains is my own.

The capitalists will supply us with the materials and technology which we lack and will restore our military industry which we need for our future victorious attacks upon our suppliers. In other words, they will work hard in order to prepare their own suicides.
—Lenin, *Memorandum to Chicherin*, 1921

THE DOUBLE-CROSS CIRCUIT

One

Night comes early in Aubervilliers. For the inhabitants of this working-class suburb to the northeast of Paris rise long before dawn. It's been this way since the early days of the factory system, and despite many fervent hopes to the contrary the system has not changed very much.

So there were not many people to be seen as the man walked west from l'avenue de la République along la rue Sadi Carnot. Several Arabs hurried past him with frowns on their faces. A blonde girl in a short sheepskin jacket gazed at him a moment with a professional eye, but she could see that his coat was threadbare.

It wasn't just his coat, though the velvet collar that smacked of former wealth now made him seem merely pathetic. His entire being was threadbare—from the large vacant eyes to the small battered suitcase of yellow cardboard.

He didn't walk. There was no energy left in his legs

for him to lift his feet. He slid along the sidewalk like an old newspaper blown by the wind. Yet he kept his eyes turned up toward the façades of the buildings. He was seeking something.

The alley was so narrow that a man in a hurry would have missed it. Not he. His worn shoe hung over the lip of the sidewalk. He looked for the street sign and saw that the alley was named ruelle de la Sauvegarde. It gave onto a small courtyard. The courtyard was dark but for a blue neon light that flickered to the left.

Turning, he began to walk toward the blue light.

It was the light of l'Hôtel la Tourmente, once a respectable family-run establishment where commercial travelers spent the night before proceeding into Paris proper. That was long ago. Now it was in its terminal phase: a *maison de passe* where the local girls brought their daytime customers.

The staff didn't even know who owned the hotel nowadays. Once a month a man appeared with their pay envelopes and his looks did not invite questions. The staff didn't care anyway—so long as they were paid. There were only three of them now: the day clerk, the night clerk, and the woman who cleaned the rooms once a week.

The night clerk was fast asleep when the tired man with the suitcase pulled the bell. It took the night clerk a while to rouse himself, turn on the light in the hall, and unlock the front door.

"What do you want?" The night clerk had a bad cold and stared at the man through rheumy eyelids.

"A room."

The night clerk peered suspiciously at the man. Real clients rarely came to La Tourmente any more.

"Oh all right," the clerk said sourly, pulling the door wide, "but you have to pay in advance."

THE DOUBLE-CROSS CIRCUIT

The man followed the clerk to the desk. The clerk leaned over and unhooked a key from the board.

"Room 25. That's the second floor. The light's by the stairs. It's fifteen francs."

The man handed him a crumpled bill. The clerk unfolded it, saw it was a twenty, and, grumbling, went to his office to get the change. When he returned, the man had already gone up. The clerk shrugged.

"Monsieur, if you don't care, I don't care." He put the five franc piece into his pocket and returned to the office to go back to sleep.

The room was poor but neat. It contained a bed, a table, a chair, and a sink. There were no towels on the single-bar rack. The man placed his suitcase on the bed, then sat down on the chair. He did not remove his coat. He stared into his palms. Suddenly he began to weep.

It was soundless crying. The tears ran down his cheeks, along the deep lines by the side of his mouth. From time to time he sucked in air as though he were choking.

The moisture in his eyes made them seem less dull, less foggy. For a moment, his expression lost its yellow lifelessness. His face had the ravaged look of one who still hopes even after prolonged physical or spiritual torment. Momentarily his eyes seemed to glow, then the dullness returned. The tears stopped.

He stood, crossed over to the bed, and opened the suitcase. He took out a bottle. He closed the suitcase. But this time he turned it so that the snaps, instead of facing the foot of the bed, faced to the right. The bottle had not yet been opened. It contained Pernod: the cheapest available brand. He twisted the cap off and, standing in the middle of the room, drank, gulping the stuff down undiluted.

When the bottle was two-thirds empty, he put it down on a corner of the table. His face now had a dazed, passive air. Nearly polite, as though he were awaiting the answer to a question.

It did not take long. As always, the pain was blinding. His lips twisted in an atrocious grimace as he sank to his knees, both hands tightly clasped to his abdomen. His vomiting was violent but brief. A watery green fluid, reeking of Pernod, now formed a small pool on the floor.

He waited, doubled over, until the attack had passed. His face had gone white. Slowly he straightened up and wiped his mouth with the back of his hand.

He got to his feet and sat down at the table.

The table had a single drawer. He pulled it open. The drawer was empty save for a sheet of paper lining the bottom. He lifted out the paper and placed it flat on the tabletop. He stared at the paper. His hand reached for the bottle once more. He emptied it rapidly.

He unbuttoned his coat. Under it he wore a frayed blue suit. From the breast pocket protruded a ball-point pen. He uncapped the pen and began making a series of quick lines upon the paper. With his right hand he clutched at his stomach. The awful searing pain was returning. A greasy film of sweat had broken over his face. Biting his lip, he continued to mark the sheet of paper. His hand had begun to shake uncontrollably.

A groan of agony tore from his throat. He bent forward, banging his face against the table. A trickle of blood dripped from his nose onto the paper.

Knocking back the chair, he lurched toward the bed. He fell on his knees before the yellow suitcase. One hand grabbed at the fasteners; the other tore at his liver, trying to still the excruciating ache.

The suitcase lid popped open. His free hand rum-

THE DOUBLE-CROSS CIRCUIT

maged within and finally closed around the revolver. It was a Smith & Wesson .38. World War II vintage. It shook as he tried to get a grip on it.

He turned the gun toward himself. The pain was numbing his fingers. His breathing came hard and rapid. He let go of his side, attempting to get both hands on the gun. His mouth moved, twisting over the words.

"Oh God, forgive me!"

He tried to shout, but it came only as a hoarse croak. The words were in American English.

He lifted the gun, arms before him clasped as though in prayer.

He pulled the gun toward his face. The barrel broke one of his front teeth as he forced it into his mouth. Two fingers squeezed the trigger.

The explosion puffed out his cheeks and the force of the emerging bullet thrust him forward. He fell slowly as the final dullness glazed his eyes. His face tumbled into the suitcase on the bed. The lid quivered, but remained open.

In the office two floors below, the night clerk stirred uneasily in his sleep but did not wake. There was no one else in l'Hôtel la Tourmente.

At 7:15 the following morning, the night clerk's alarm rang. Ten minutes later, he locked the front door and wandered off for *café-croissants* at the bistro near his home.

At 8:30, the day clerk arrived. He didn't bother to check the keyboard. If any customers had come—which wasn't very likely—the night clerk would have made them pay beforehand. The day clerk finished reading his morning paper, then curled up on the leather couch in the office, the one vacated by the night clerk seventy-five minutes earlier.

It was just after 10:30 when Marie-Thérèse Raquin, who cleaned the rooms at La Tourmente once a week, appeared. By a quarter to eleven, she had finished gossiping with the day clerk, now fully awake and seated behind the desk. She changed into her felt slippers and set about on the first floor rooms.

It was almost one when Marie-Thérèse gave a piercing scream.

That day was a black one for La Tourmente. The girls who arrived, customers in tow, took one look at the black-and-white police van and car parked in front and knew the time had come to find another hotel. And the police in the course of their investigation discovered that the hotel belonged to a man for whom the Anti-Gang Squad had a warrant. One week after the suicide, La Tourmente would be for sale and the ex-staff would for a long time afterward curse the man in room 25. But these developments are another matter altogether ...

Inside room 25, the morgue photographer snapped his case shut.

"Okay, chief, I'm through."

The inspector nodded. He addressed the uniformed policeman by the door.

"Tell the print boys they can come in now."

Inspector Verrier moved aside as the print men began dusting. He stared at the kneeling form of the dead man and pursed his lips. Within five minutes of having entered the room, the inspector had seen this case go from the watertight obvious to ... to ... He didn't know.

He had looked around. It had seemed clear-cut. The

THE DOUBLE-CROSS CIRCUIT 7

man's worn appearance, the bottle, the gun. Certainly nothing extraordinary.

Then he had patted the man's clothes. There were no identification papers. In itself, that wasn't terribly unusual either. The fellow probably hadn't wanted to embarrass his family. Suicides often showed curious scruples.

He had looked in the suitcase. What with the man's head and the blood it was hard to tell what else was in there. That would have to wait for the lab.

And in a place like this one, there were no hotel cards either.

So, Verrier reasoned, he had a John Doe on his hands. This led him to look inside the man's jacket. Given the man's kneeling position, this had not been easy to do. The inspector was looking for a clothing label. There was none. The label had been carefully removed.

The inspector was left with the unpleasant thought that this John Doe had gone to some lengths to conceal his identity. He was almost sure there wasn't a single identifying mark on the rest of the man's clothes. But he couldn't be absolutely certain until the corpse was undressed and the clothes examined.

This secrecy annoyed the inspector. His work was already difficult enough. Then he found the paper on the desk. And from that point, Verrier knew he was going to have problems with this case.

As the fingerprint men worked their way around the room, the inspector once again looked down at the piece of paper. The lines formed a shape as though the man had tried to draw something. He hadn't succeeded. Or, rather, Verrier could not identify the shape. Across this form, the dead man had written in a very shaky hand a single word.

The inspector read the word again. As though by repeating it enough, he would at last grasp what it was supposed to mean.

The word written by the dead man in room 25 was UNICOM.

Two

In the middle of St. Giles' Circus, London, there stands a high office tower of aluminum and glass named Centre Place. A very prime piece of real estate, it is the only major London property owned by a company called CONSERV, S.A., which occupies the eighteenth and nineteenth floors of the building.

To the other companies that rent office space in the tower, CONSERV, S.A. is simply a sort of corporate landlord.

One could scarcely be more wrong.

CONSERV is a very special kind of company. It is not listed on the London Stock Exchange—or any other exchange. In fact, its legal existence is carefully concealed behind numerous smoke screens. But if you could penetrate some of the mumbo jumbo behind which CONSERV shields itself, you would find some interesting information.

For instance, that CONSERV is a company registered

in Liechtenstein. From this fact alone two conclusions follow. One, that CONSERV does not like to pay taxes, which could lead to the suspicion that the company realizes fantastic profits. And two, that CONSERV prefers to keep a veil drawn over the nature of its business.

But if you continued to dig, with some luck you would eventually discover that CONSERV is owned by another company whose British headquarters are not a half-mile from Centre Place. In Aldwych, surrounded by insurance companies. For CONSERV's parent company is Global Telephone & Telegraph, the huge, highly successful communications multinational with branches in over seventy countries. You would also discover that CONSERV's director-general, Nicolas A. Ross, is a member of the board of directors of GTT.

And if you were left wondering what could be the connection between highly visible and well-established GTT and secretive CONSERV, the answer would have to be that business, like the Lord, works in mysterious ways.

Nicolas Ross paced around the large office on the eighteenth floor of Centre Place. Below, Tottenham Court Road stretched into Euston. All the buildings at ground level seemed diminutive. The only other construction of a comparable size nearby was the Government Post Office Tower with its necklace of microwave amplifiers.

Nicolas Ross was a small, neat man with short gray hair and bushy black eyebrows. He was in his mid-sixties but his nervous staccato movements had the energy of a much younger man. He was in his shirt-sleeves; on each arm he wore a band of flexible stainless steel that kept him from getting ink on his shirt cuffs. The jacket of his dark-gray suit was neatly hung against the door.

THE DOUBLE-CROSS CIRCUIT

the Russians we were prepared to share UNICOM with them, it would go a long way toward convincing them of our good will."

"Good will?" Hong snorted. "I can think of certain quarters where such an action would be considered treasonable."

Nicolas Ross leaned back in his chair.

"Gentlemen, before there is a further unnecessary display of emotion, I have two details of which I should like to apprise you. The first is this: it had occurred to me before that Tomas might encounter difficulties in the course of the negotiations. Indeed, as he explained to you, these have materialized. The problem—the only problem—is how best to overcome the obstacles in our way.

"In other words, we require a convincing bargaining counter that can overrule any hesitation we meet from the Russians. As it happens, we do possess such a bargaining counter in the UNICOM.

"Second, as William has just indicated obscurely, there is the matter of the National Security Act. It does not apply to us since CONSERV is not an American company, but it does govern GTT's trading arrangements and so should be taken into account. According to the National Security Act, the American government has final approval over the business transactions of U.S.-registered corporations in their dealings with the Eastern bloc countries.

"I have checked with Central Intelligence and they have approved the operation. To that end, I directed Dr. Vardney to modify the UNICOM in such a way that, should we offer it to the Russians, they will be able to intercept only those NATO communications we allow them to.

"I trust this information will allay whatever doubts you might have had on those points. Unless there are any further objections, may we consider the matter decided upon?"

So it was agreed that the negotiations in Moscow would be revived with an offer of access into NATO's new communications system.

"Tomas," Ross asked, "when's your next meeting with the SCST?"

"Two days from now," Herscu replied.

"Very well. You'll put it to the chairman, Gvashvili, in person and in private. I don't want Hendersley to know about this." Hendersley was the GTT representative on the CONSERV negotiating team. "And I want daily calls from you after you've spoken with Chairman Gvashvili.

"The rest of you carry on. You may mention to interested clients that we're working on new systems that'll have a major impact. Nothing concrete, though—just enough to stir up their interest."

Ross threw down the pencil with which he had been making notes. The meeting was over.

After the directors had gone, Nicolas Ross walked over to the window—a wall of glass from floor to ceiling affording a commanding view of London below. It was, in the military analogy he preferred, like a command post giving him access to the city at his feet. In fact, he saw the relationship between CONSERV and GTT as that of a commando unit to the main army corps. CONSERV was the commando, parachuted behind enemy lines to map out the weak points in enemy defenses, to discover and secure and facilitate the entry of the main invasion force into the target territory.

Another term could also be applied to CONSERV—it was GTT's Fifth Column. From the day CONSERV came into being, it had one mandate: to find markets; to

By training, Nicolas Ross was an engineer. By the workings of reality, he was one of the most powerful men in the contemporary world. Yet his name was almost completely unknown.

His renown came entirely from the company he had created and whose moving spirit he was: CONSERV. For though CONSERV—except to a select few—meant as little within European and American business circles as did the name Ross, this was not the case in South America, in Africa, and in Asia.

There was a quiet rap on the door. A dark-haired young man stood in the doorway. The cut of his beige suit was almost perfect. Only a trained eye would have detected the slight bulge of the gun by the right armpit.

"They are here, sir."

"Fine, Harris. Show them in." Ross had never lost the American accent inherited from his father.

They were four: the regional directors for Asia, Africa, South America, and the Communist bloc. By their names: William Hong, Belkacem Sa'ab, Ernesto Schneider, and Tomas Herscu. All engineers. Nicolas Ross, in addition to being director-general, was regional director for North America and Europe.

The regional directors took their seats around the oval table that occupied the left half of Ross's office. Nicolas Ross did not bother to put on his jacket before he too seated himself.

"Gentlemen, good morning. I have called this meeting of the directors at the request of Mr. Tomas Herscu. That said, I will let him expose to you the situation we now face."

All eyes turned toward the slender, fair-haired Rumanian.

"Mr. Ross . . . gentlemen," Herscu began, speaking softly with a faint British lilt, "for the past several months I have been in Moscow negotiating with the members of the Soviet State Committee for Science and Technology. The object of our discussions, the objective, is the largest contract ever signed between the Soviet government and a Western company. . . ."

There was an animated murmur from the other directors—except for Ross, whose face was expressionless. Herscu waited until the excitement subsided, then resumed.

"We are speaking here of a contract worth approximately one billion dollars for each of the five years of its duration, with the possibility of renewing it if the Russians prove satisfied with our work.

"The undertaking is nonmilitary. As a first step, it involves completely redesigning Aeroflot's internal communications systems, to be followed with a second communications system for the State Planning Committee which centralizes the economic life of the Soviet Union.

"There's no need for me to stress what an opportunity this represents for us. Built into this contract are further possibilities which as recently as two years ago were inconceivable.

"However, I am certain that the advantages are obvious to you. If only my report could be restricted to the positive aspects. Unfortunately, that is not the case."

Herscu paused and looked at the other directors before continuing.

"Until last week, I would have reported to you that our negotiations were going well. Any dealing with the Russians operates on a great many levels. Even when

THE DOUBLE-CROSS CIRCUIT

the Russians we were prepared to share UNICOM with them, it would go a long way toward convincing them of our good will."

"Good will?" Hong snorted. "I can think of certain quarters where such an action would be considered treasonable."

Nicolas Ross leaned back in his chair.

"Gentlemen, before there is a further unnecessary display of emotion, I have two details of which I should like to apprise you. The first is this: it had occurred to me before that Tomas might encounter difficulties in the course of the negotiations. Indeed, as he explained to you, these have materialized. The problem—the only problem—is how best to overcome the obstacles in our way.

"In other words, we require a convincing bargaining counter that can overrule any hesitation we meet from the Russians. As it happens, we do possess such a bargaining counter in the UNICOM.

"Second, as William has just indicated obscurely, there is the matter of the National Security Act. It does not apply to us since CONSERV is not an American company, but it does govern GTT's trading arrangements and so should be taken into account. According to the National Security Act, the American government has final approval over the business transactions of U.S.-registered corporations in their dealings with the Eastern bloc countries.

"I have checked with Central Intelligence and they have approved the operation. To that end, I directed Dr. Vardney to modify the UNICOM in such a way that, should we offer it to the Russians, they will be able to intercept only those NATO communications we allow them to.

"I trust this information will allay whatever doubts you might have had on those points. Unless there are any further objections, may we consider the matter decided upon?"

So it was agreed that the negotiations in Moscow would be revived with an offer of access into NATO's new communications system.

"Tomas," Ross asked, "when's your next meeting with the SCST?"

"Two days from now," Herscu replied.

"Very well. You'll put it to the chairman, Gvashvili, in person and in private. I don't want Hendersley to know about this." Hendersley was the GTT representative on the CONSERV negotiating team. "And I want daily calls from you after you've spoken with Chairman Gvashvili.

"The rest of you carry on. You may mention to interested clients that we're working on new systems that'll have a major impact. Nothing concrete, though—just enough to stir up their interest."

Ross threw down the pencil with which he had been making notes. The meeting was over.

After the directors had gone, Nicolas Ross walked over to the window—a wall of glass from floor to ceiling affording a commanding view of London below. It was, in the military analogy he preferred, like a command post giving him access to the city at his feet. In fact, he saw the relationship between CONSERV and GTT as that of a commando unit to the main army corps. CONSERV was the commando, parachuted behind enemy lines to map out the weak points in enemy defenses, to discover and secure and facilitate the entry of the main invasion force into the target territory.

Another term could also be applied to CONSERV—it was GTT's Fifth Column. From the day CONSERV came into being, it had one mandate: to find markets; to they say nothing to you, they manage to communicate whether or not you are finding favor in their eyes.

"To give you one example: we can judge how receptive the Russians are to a project simply by the kind of room in which they choose to conduct their deliberations with you. Until last week, we had nothing to complain about. Then suddenly, without notice, they moved the negotiations to a godforsaken ministry on the outskirts of Moscow. I questioned the head of the SCST, Dr. Matvei Gvashvili, about this. His only reply was that Westerners were too accustomed to 'bourgeois living.'

"It is one example of many. But the indications I am getting are not encouraging. They appear to have lost interest in our project, possibly as a result of a conflict within the Politburo over doing business with us on the scale we have proposed.

"Gentlemen, I am afraid we are going to lose that contract. The reason I asked for this meeting is so that we can come up with something convincing enough to persuade the Russians they have everything to gain from signing with us."

Tomas Herscu took a sip from the glass of water before him. He had finished.

Nicolas Ross looked at the other directors.

"Well, gentlemen?" he said, bushy eyebrows raised expectantly.

William Hong was the first to speak. Hong had a trait rare in a Chinese—Taiwanese, really. He had blue eyes.

"Tomas, you are in effect suggesting we bribe the Russians?" Hong spoke with a Boston accent, a residue of his years at MIT.

"If that's what you wish to call it, Bill, though they aren't interested in money as such," Herscu answered.

"Come, come," Ross interjected, "it's solutions we need, not word games. Ernesto?"

Schneider, the Chilean, shrugged, then shook his head. He was still trying to obtain compensation from the Pinochet government for the GTT properties nationalized under Allende. The problems in his area were such that he had little energy left for those of the other directors.

Ross made a mark on the legal-size pad next to him.

"Belkacem? You haven't said anything."

Belkacem Sa'ab was the man who had launched CONSERV's spearhead into North Africa, beginning with the first huge contract for the reorganization of newly independent Algeria's telephone system in 1964.

"The situation in my area being what it is, we are still not sufficiently consolidated to be able to offer anything on the scale required. I think we have to turn to our more established markets here and you, Nicolas, I believe, have in your possession an article which might greatly interest the Russians."

"Yes, Belkacem?"

"I'm referring to the NATO UNICOM."

An air of satisfaction showed in Nicolas Ross's eyes. He looked at Herscu across the table.

"How would the Russians respond if you offered them the secrets to the NATO UNICOM? I refer the rest of you to our contract EUR VSM (d) 699 207 331 for the design and installation before the end of the year of the central component for a totally impenetrable communications security system."

There was a rustling of papers as the directors not directly concerned consulted the folders before them.

"The contract with NATO was signed before our negotiations with the Russians began. In truth, at the time of the signature of the NATO contract, it did not seem that the progress that materialized subsequently with the Russians would be likely for some time," Ross explained.

"Yes," Herscu said decisively, "I think if I indicated to

THE DOUBLE-CROSS CIRCUIT 17

create demand for GTT products; to feed the vast industrial organization of GTT's factories.

When CONSERV came into existence, Europe lay in the ruins caused by World War II. American and British businesses poured into a prostrate Europe, eager to profit from the devastation. Fast-buck artists made a killing.

Nicolas Ross was not one of these. He was not interested in quick money, in temporary demand that would soon dry up. He was interested in the future.

He had digested the lessons of the war, and he was one of the first who could clearly spell out the writing in blood on the shell-shattered walls. Germany under Hitler had only attempted to repeat Britain's and France's colonial expansion. Geography and the USSR had stopped her. In attempting to destroy the Hitlerian menace, Britain and France had driven hammer blows into the very foundations of their own empires. The cracks were everywhere, and through the cracks Nicolas Ross could see the future.

It took twenty years for a name to be given to that which Ross had first seen right after the war. Decolonization. And by the time—by the early sixties—the decolonization process turned into an avalanche, CONSERV was already firmly implanted.

Newly emerged nations have an interesting sense of vanity. Especially if relations with the former metropolitan nation get off to a bad start.

Ross knew how to play upon the vanities of the new leaders. He came to know a lot about the mentalities of guerilla fighters. And it meant something to those poor devils living in the bush, fighting seemingly hopeless wars of attrition, ill-equipped, badly armed, to be sought out by CONSERV and given even then the consideration extended to heads of state. They never forgot it. And so many did become the heads of state of their new nations. Then CONSERV returned to claim its reward.

"We have them by their telephones," Ross was once heard to joke—in a rare moment of levity. But it was true. The new countries wanted nothing but the best. Even when they didn't have the facilities. CONSERV would provide—private lines, switching systems, intercoms. All kinds of electronic marvels for the new rulers to play with.

It was amusing at first. Then it ceased to be funny. In Ghana, for instance, while Nkrumah frolicked beside his Olympic-size pool next to his palace wired with stereo speakers in every room, people were starving beyond the electrified fences.

The logic which CONSERV represented advanced another step. There were coups d'etat; new men emerged and these weren't interested in toys. They wanted radar systems, armaments, teleguidance systems for missiles. Their armies needed new equipment; the nation needed a development plan. Everything was to be modernized and improved. A country wasn't a real country unless there was a telephone in every home.

Development went ahead. And the larger the development allocations, the more intense the power struggles behind the scenes. Newly created secret services required special installations.

Implacably, the process continued. Special telephone facilities weren't enough; there were enemies to repress. The reports of torture ceased to be individual stories; repression became systematic.

In Brazil, along with the development of TeleBras, the national telephone company, grew the torture camps and murder squads.

In Chile, Allende dared try to nationalize the GTT-owned telephone company. He was destroyed during the coup d'etat by which a right-wing military dictatorship came to power.

In country after country, the CONSERV representative was seen in the company of the heads of the secret police. In Chile, the DINA. In Venezuela, the DISIP. In South Africa, BOSS. In Rhodesia, the SSS. In Iran, SAVAK. In Korea, the KCIA.

It was not that CONSERV had preferences. But it had to be recognized that repressive, military regimes were very good customers.

And yet CONSERV wanted nothing better than to do business with the other side as well. In Cuba, for instance, the facilities there had once been owned—before Castro—by the company that became GTT. The equipment was American-made and there was almost a sentimental desire to return to old haunts. Also, unable to replace their stock, the Cuban telephone system was degenerating rapidly. CONSERV was optimistic that Cuba would soon count among its clients.

In Vietnam, during the days of the Republic, CONSERV had done considerable work reorganizing the telephone system both for the U.S. Army and the Saigon government. Since unification of north and south, Hanoi had not been able to make use of much of the southern system. Here, too, CONSERV knew that a call was but a matter of time.

But the real jewel in the crown was the Russian deal. If the negotiations worked out, Russia would be signing with CONSERV, on behalf of GTT, the biggest contract ever made with a capitalist firm. That was why it was so important that the negotiations be successfuly completed.

Nicolas Ross finished his rapid *tour d'horizon* of CONSERV's past. His eyes fixed on the three telephones upon his desk, and for a moment he was carried on a wave of nostalgia. The sudden ringing of one of the phones startled him back to the present.

Ross reached for the middle phone. This was connected to GTT's private network, which meant that Ross could call anywhere within company territory in England, Europe, and America without having to go outside the GTT system.

"Nicolas Ross here."

"It's Hutchins at the School, sir." Jack Hutchins was research director at the GTT-owned property in Bletchley Park, north of London. Known within the company as "the School," the red brick house in Bletchley Park was the place where the British Secret Service kept its famous Ultra cipher machine during the war.

Smuggled into Britain before the outbreak of the war by a courageous Polish spy, Ultra enabled the Allies to read the German High Command's supposedly unbreakable code throughout the duration of the conflict. The Germans never found out. After the war, the house and grounds were bought by GTT. The poverty-stricken British government was pleased with the large sum paid for the property.

Hutchins sounded very nervous.

"Yes, Hutch, what is it?"

"I should have known, Mr. Ross, when he didn't return. But I assumed he'd gone on another of his benders. You know, sometimes, they'd last two weeks. I . . . I just didn't think. . . ."

"What the hell are you going on about? Make sense, man!"

"It's Vardney, Mr. Ross. He's disappeared!"

Nicolas Ross's face slowly went white.

"I'll be right over! Do not touch a thing until I arrive."

Three

A DEAD MAN can tell you a great many things about himself. Sometimes, though, these aren't the things you want to know. Such was the case with the tired man who shot himself in room 25.

His body was taken—in a rubberized bag with a zipper down the front—to l'Institut Médico-Légal, a cavernous building near la Gare d'Austerlitz. It is here, where everything smells of formaldehyde, that some of the best police work in France is performed.

The man's body was laid out in one of the examining rooms in the subbasement. A white-tiled room in whose center was a waist-high marble block that bore a slight resemblance to Napoleon's Tomb in Les Invalides. By the head of the block was a sink. A tangle of thin hoses was connected to the taps.

The dead man was still in his clothes. His sightless

eyes—the left one partially closed in a macabre wink—stared vacantly at the ceiling.

Two preliminary tests were run. The first was a simple blood test to make certain that the blood coagulating in the man's veins matched that of the fatal head wound. This might have seemed unnecessary, but the pathologists never took anything for granted. Even the obvious. The blood matched.

Next, a wax imprint was taken of the man's fingertips. To check for powder burns and so be certain that the man had indeed pulled the trigger. Apparently he had. Unless any evidence emerged to suggest the contrary, it now seemed clear that the man's death was self-inflicted.

The examining pathologist made a notation on his clipboard. Then he turned to his assistant.

"All right, remove his clothes and have them sent up to Forensic. After that, wash around the wound but do so very carefully. Tell me when you're ready and we'll take a look inside."

The pathologist walked toward the wall against which the inspector from Aubervilliers was leaning. The inspector was smoking thoughtfully.

"So?" the pathologist asked.

"Found him in a flea-pit hotel room. A suicide. No papers. I can't tell you anything more. I'm hoping you can tell me that. Cigarette?"

"Thanks." The pathologist leaned forward as the inspector flicked his lighter. "Stick around then. We'll get going in a minute. Do you want a photograph before we carve him up?"

Inspector Verrier nodded.

A little over two hours later, the dead man was no longer recognizable. He had been gutted like a fish. Just above his ears, the skull had been removed. The cheeks laid open. A hole ran from his sternum to his crotch.

The inspector watched fascinated while the two pathologists cut, sawed, probed, removed, weighed, and marked. Verrier saw the man's brain minus what the bullet had torn off carefully weighed on a scale. A disgusting thing supposed to be the man's liver had also been lengthily peered at. He had gazed curiously at the blackened lungs. The fetid odors that filled the room reminded him of a slaughterhouse, and yet his own profound interest in what was going on kept him from lapsing too deeply into melancholy. Still, he was conscious of a numb sadness within. If men were not so filled with secrets, there would be no need to look into their guts to try to understand what transpired in their minds.

The two pathologists worked in silence, punctuated only by the metallic clatter of their instruments and an occasional knowledgeable grunt.

Finally, the chief pathologist straightened up and peeled off his gloves. He made several more notations on his clipboard, then carefully washed his hands and forearms. He came toward the inspector who was suddenly very conscious of the bloody smears on the doctor's smock.

"Can I have another of your fags? Seem to have lost mine."

The inspector gave him one of his, a Disque Bleu. The doctor snorted out the smoke through his nostrils.

"Well, what can I tell you? Cause of death: a massive brain hemorrhage brought on by the passage of the bullet, but I'm sure that's no surprise.

"What surprised me was that the fellow even got a chance to do himself in. Christ, what a wreck! There were three other things that could have killed him at any instant. For one, his liver. It was so bloated with poison—any day it could have ruptured and that would have been that. For another, his teeth. I don't think he'd seen a dentist in thirty years. All his teeth, those that remained, were rotten. Pus from his teeth had collected under his jaw. There, too, it could have gotten into his bloodstream at any point. Third, his heart. Enlarged. The arteries badly clogged. He'd had one coronary several years ago: the left ventricle was scarred. He was a prime candidate for another and fatal heart attack. In all, it's miraculous that he lived long enough to shoot himself.

"I can tell you he lived a completely sedentary life. The spine is distorted from too much sitting. Also his hands are not callused.

"He smoked too much." The pathologist looked wryly at his cigarette. "And he was a chronic alcoholic. For what it's worth, his brain was larger than normal. Compensating for what the bullet destroyed, his brain was above average in size. That could mean, if you consider his stooped posture and the lack of calluses on his hands, he was an intellectual. But then a large brain needn't necessarily mean anything at all. That's about it, I'm afraid."

He scowled at the disappointment he saw on the inspector's face.

"That's all? No idea as to nationality?"

"I had hoped that his dental work might provide an indication. As I said, the teeth that remained were too rotten and what fillings there were are too old for me even to guess. He could be French; he could be Australian." The pathologist shrugged. "Sorry. You'll get a copy of my report, but I've mentioned the most significant points."

Verrier sighed.

"Okay, thanks, Doc."

As he left, he took a last look at the corpse. He was beginning to dislike his mysterious John Doe. There was

THE DOUBLE-CROSS CIRCUIT 25

nothing to do now but wait for the results from the forensic lab.

And these only confirmed what the inspector had guessed at in room 25. There was not a clothing label anywhere. The man had worn no underwear. His socks were too full of holes for there to be a trace of the manufacturer's stamp. The shoes too. The lab guessed they might be Italian, but noted that there were too many imitation brands today to be certain. The man's suit was of Taiwanese weave and mass-manufactured. No idea where—could have been Canada, or Taiwan, or the United States, or Europe. The overcoat was English, but coats like this were sold everywhere. The tie obviously secondhand.

The man's suitcase was a cheap sort of the kind made in Hungary. Sold in any large department store. Inside the suitcase was a bunch of old newspaper pages. No other personal effects.

Microscopic analysis revealed traces of dirt. Paris dirt and non-Paris dirt. Pieces of fluff on the man's coat showed that he had ridden in a car within the last month. A Renault. It could have been a taxi or a private car.

The man's pockets produced traces of tobacco—British, American, and French. Also bread crumbs. And Frs. 35,70 in notes and coins.

Ballistics reported that the .38 was untraceable. There were simply too many like it in circulation. The same applied to the ammunition.

In other words, there was nothing to go on. A big fat zero. The inspector tossed the reports onto his desk.

"Merde! Et double merde!"

His colleagues in the Aubervilliers Commissariat's Department of Criminal Investigations looked at him askance. They liked it when "the Bloodhound" ran into difficulties. Now he knew how they felt most of the time. Frustrated.

He got up from his desk and went to the bathroom. When he returned, he lit another Disque Bleu and once again picked up the lab reports.

The age of the newspapers found in the man's suitcase varied from three weeks to two months. None of the articles seemed to bear any relevance. The dates formed no particular squence. And yet the man had marked certain letters appearing in the articles: the *U*s . . . the *N*s . . . the *I*s . . . *C*s . . . the *O*s . . . the *M*s.

UNICOM.

Again

Once the newspaper pages, the word formed a repetitive crossword puzzle. An obsessive litany. UNICOM. Vertically. Horizontally. Transversally. The same word as on the sheet of paper with the formless drawing.

He took a pad of paper from his desk drawer and began writing the word forward and backward.

"Verrier!"

Engrossed, he did not hear his name.

"Verrier!"

He looked up, startled. His chief was glowering at him from the doorway of his office.

Martinelli, the chief of detectives, carried his gun in the small of his back. The joke in the Commissariat was that he'd got the idea from watching an old Mike Connors program on *la télé*. But then it didn't make much difference where Martinelli carried his gun since he never used it. He was a bureaucrat first and a cop second.

Verrier sat down on the chair near the chief's desk. Martinelli pushed a packet of Marlboros toward him. The inspector declined.

"So how's it going with your John Doe?"

The inspector made a face.

"I see. Do you think you can wrap it up in the next couple of days?"

"No way."

"Very well, then. Stamp it 'unsolved' and give me the file."

Verrier felt his cheeks flush angrily.

"What the hell for?"

Martinelli looked at him a moment and shook his head.

"There's an ill wind blowing through the Préfecture. The new under-prefect—the one who went to school in the States—is wild on efficiency. The word is a big crackdown is going to happen soon. The under-prefect has the nod from the Minister who is under pressure in the Chamber because public opinion has once again turned against us. Jesus, a few civilians are accidentally shot in the course of investigations and the entire police administration comes under suspicion!"

He was referring to the outcry in the national press which had followed an undercover squad's recent shooting of six bystanders on the Champs-Elysées during a chase after a bank robbery. The "incident" had resulted in the appointment of the new under-prefect of police.

"So this young hot-shot has the green light to turn the PJ into a model of efficiency and the Minister, armed with facts, can then shout down the Communist accusations in the Chamber."

The inspector stared stonily at his chief. Departmental politics were, as always, utterly Byzantine.

"The under-prefect," Martinelli went on sententiously, "feels that the high number of unsolved cases in the last months stems from police laziness. He has vowed to reduce the percentages by twenty-five points across the board. And we're going to help him . . . ," Martinelli smiled, "by letting him break his teeth.

"You see, if a guy like you is having problems with a case, do you really think those idiots downtown will do any better? They're welcome to try! We'll see who laughs last.

"So we're sending them only the Unsolveds of our best men. That's why I asked you about your John Doe. Let them have a go at it. They'll see soon enough what it's really like and then they'll leave us alone.

"You'll bring me the file, then? After they've mucked around with it a bit and gotten nowhere, you'll get it back. With apologies!" Martinelli raised a pudgy finger.

"Fat lot of good they'll do me," the inspector murmured.

"You'll get it back. Just a question of time," Martinelli said reassuringly.

He was wrong. Inspector Verrier would never see the file on "his" John Doe again.

The inspector returned to his desk and closed the file. He picked up the UNSOLVED stamp, breathed on it, and smashed it savagely on the folder cover.

In one way, he was not sorry to see it taken from him. He was too experienced a cop not to recognize a first-class pain in the ass of a case. And then in another way, he regretted he would not be able to work out why the man in room 25 had killed himself. He knew full well that by the time the file was returned the trail would have grown too cold. Still, he felt regretful. He was too good a cop not to be annoyed that it was going before he had finished with it. There was something about this case . . .

". . . And look at this one, *Monsieur le Préfet*," said the under-prefect of police, "from Aubervilliers-Centre! It's a veritable scandal. One man, a clear-cut suicide, and they file it as 'Unsolved.' No, really, this is too much...."

The old prefect looked with distaste at the younger man, his files scattered about him on the highly polished table. One of the prefect's eyebrows arched in surprise.

"Surely, Gervais, you're exaggerating. This is absurd."

"See for yourself, *M. le Préfet*," Gervais replied, stretching forth his arm to present the file. The prefect noticed that Gervais had clear polish on his fingernails. He felt a pang of irritation.

"Hm," grunted the prefect as he leafed through the file. "You may have a point. This is certainly careless on their part."

"Careless, *M. le Préfet*," Gervais exclaimed. "This is hardly carelessness, it's..."

"Yes, yes, I know, a scandal," the old prefect sighed, holding up his hand. Behind the younger man, he could see the bright daylight outside and, in the distance, the radio antenna atop the Tour Eiffel.

The prefect lowered his eyes to the younger man's face.

"Well, Gervais, I'll have a look at these myself. That'll be all for the moment."

"But, *M. le Préfet*..."

"I said that would be all for now."

The old prefect watched Gervais leave. The underprefect's immaculately cut suit never showed a crease. Everything about the under-prefect profoundly annoyed the old man.

They were both so utterly different from each other. Gervais, dripping ambition from every pore, the brilliant graduate from l'Ecole Nationale d'Administration and Harvard Business School, the well-connected family background—his mother was a cousin of the current minister of the interior.... And Davoli, the prefect, a Corsican, the career policeman who'd worked his way up through the ranks, who could see so clearly in the younger man his eventual replacement. . . .

For several minutes, Davoli stared at the brightness streaming in through the windows, the gray Seine struggling to recover the green shade it had once possessed.

What galled him most was that he had to help the younger man. On that, the Minister had been quite specific. Still, the Minister had not spelled out exactly how. Davoli retained a semblance of authority in this respect.

He reached for the Aubervilliers file. Now he could examine it at his own pace without Gervais's bright eyes peering at him. He knew the men in the Commissariat there. They were neither careless nor sloppy. There had to be a reason.

Davoli opened the file and began reading about the suicide in room 25.

The human mind often seems capricious and sometimes downright frivolous. Thoughts interconnect apparently at random. An idea will join with another and they will appear to bear no relation each to each. Yet, for a moment, they do fuse; you can then either dismiss the union as ridiculous or wonder why one particular notion appears linked to the other. And it was exactly this process that set Davoli to wondering.

Reading the file, he came across the first mention of the word UNICOM and promptly the face of his friend Santerre flashed to mind. The old prefect asked himself why the one should make him think of the other. He came up with two reasons: the first being that he had lunched with Santerre two days ago and the second that an old policeman's nose had sniffed something.

Davoli looked up from the folder and frowned. Why Santerre? What had they talked about? The two men had known each other since the days of the Resistance.

THE DOUBLE-CROSS CIRCUIT

Santerre, now a colonel, worked in one of the important government agencies. What had been said two days ago?

Davoli remembered.

"Are you busy over there these days?"

Santerre had tugged at a corner of his thin mustache. "Ever since de Gaulle stepped down, we've been watching the cobwebs grow around our desks. It's still like that."

Davoli shrugged and continued reading the file.

A few minutes later, he looked up again.

No, he thought, it's not such a crazy idea. After all, the Minister said he was to help Gervais. Very well, then, he'd help Gervais. If nothing came of it, nothing was lost since Santerre's group did not have anything better to do. And if something did come of it, then the credit would be Davoli's alone—for having thought of the idea.

Davoli opened a drawer of his leather-topped desk and took out a sheet of paper. He reached for one of the three pens in the gold-plated holder.

Dear Edgar,
The enclosed came to us because our people were getting nowhere with them. Since you mentioned over lunch that your boys had nothing to do, they might find some worthwhile preoccupations among this material. After all, you are police too!

Davoli scrawled his signature at the bottom of the sheet.

He stood up, gathered together the folders which Gervais had described as "positively the worst of the lot," then placed them and his note inside a brown manila envelope.

Across the front of the envelope he scribbled Santerre's name, rank, and the address: *Colonel Edgar Santerre, Service de Documentation Extérieure et de Contre-Espionnage*, France's counterintelligence service. Davoli walked over to the door of his office and opened it.

"Here," he said to his secretary, "have this sent by despatch rider immediately."

"Tout de suite, M. le Préfet," the police officer replied, rising to his feet.

Having once more closed his door, Davoli went and stood by the window. He watched a *péniche* move slowly along the Seine. He could recall when the river had been crowded with them. Now the low barges were a rare sight.

No, he did not approve of Gervais's plans for reorganizing the work methods of the Police Judiciaire. There was another reason why he had sent the "impossible" folders to Santerre. If Santerre's people did succeed in getting anywhere with them, the resulting jealous rage within the PJ would be something to behold. Davoli was quite aware of the extent of interservice rivalries. He was also aware that by then he would have retired—he had less than a month to go. Poor Gervais would become prefect under the worst possible conditions.

Davoli smiled at the thought of Gervais's discomfiture.

Four

JACK HUTCHINS could not recall ever having known Nicolas Ross so angry.

As the research director of the School in Bletchley Park paced back and forth along the gravel drive in front of the red brick Victorian building, he could still hear Ross's furious instructions over the telephone. Hutchins was additionally angry with himself—for his meekness in the face of the director-general's unwonted display of temper. After all, it had been Ross, not Hutchins, who approved giving Vardney unrestricted access to alcohol.

Hutchins ceased pacing. For a moment he saw Vardney's face, blue eyes wild with that haunted look that had become so prominent of late.

"You poor bastard," Hutchins murmured.

He resumed his pacing, but the thought of Vardney had eradicated his anger. Now he simply felt sorry. It seemed such a waste.

Hutchins was an angular man in his late forties. With his unruly red hair and the rust-colored tweed jacket he wore constantly, he appeared very professorial. Which is what he had been before coming to GTT. Tired of the academic life, he had sought a change, doing something practical. A look of sorrow crossed Hutchins's features. His work with GTT—and particularly with CON-SERV—was practical all right. Eminently practical.

The sound of tires on gravel put an end to his musings. He looked up to see Nicolas Ross's black Rolls glide down the drive.

Ross was in no mood to indulge in trifles.

"I want to see his room."

Hutchins gazed briefly at the shorter man. Through the glasses, Ross's eyes appeared very cold and hard; black pupils with graphite irises.

"Very well, sir," Hutchins said quietly.

This part of the School was old. Beamed ceilings. A staircase that creaked. The banister dark and brightly polished, not with wax but with the passage of many hands.

The rooms where the staff lived for the duration of their stay were on the second floor. A constant draught seemed to hover in the corridor. Each room had a nameplate into which a card bearing the occupant's name was inserted. All of the rooms were kept locked.

Vardney's was room number 208.

"What's missing?" Ross asked as Hutchins unlocked the door.

"I don't know; I haven't checked."

Ross threw Hutchins an exasperated glare.

"You said not to touch a thing, sir," Hutchins said testily.

As the door swung open, the odor of vomit assailed both men's nostrils.

"Christ Almighty!" Ross swore, crossing quickly to the windows and throwing them open.

Hutchins stood by the doorway. The room looked as though it had been ransacked. Clothes were strewn about; books ripped apart; the paintings on the walls tilted wildly. There was vomit and blood on the sheets of the unmade bed. Another foul smell reached them both. Hutchins glanced around and saw human excrement in a corner.

"The poor pathetic bastard!" Hutchins cried out angrily.

Ross looked at him unemotionally.

"Has anyone unauthorized been in here?"

"Only Vardney. As I said when I called you, I looked in. That was all."

"Leave me alone here. I'll see you in the lab in a half-hour or so."

As Hutchins left, Ross asked him to shut the door.

Ross carefully scanned the room.

What a filthy sonovabitch, that Vardney. For if no one had entered except Hutchins who just looked around, then all this mess was his. This room seems to have been searched. Why was Vardney searching his own room?

Ross let the question trickle through his mind.

What had Vardney hidden in this room?

In one rapid motion, Ross moved to the bed. He grabbed the sheets and blanket, ripped them off the mattress, and threw the lot onto the floor. He began to pat the mattress, feeling for lumps. When he had done the topside, he turned the mattress over and examined the underside.

Nothing.

He rolled up the mattress and stared at the bedframe.

It consisted of springs mounted on tubular legs. Kneeling on the springs, Ross peered closely at the frame, searching for any signs of scrapes in the metal—something to indicate that the frame had recently been tampered with.
Nothing.
One by one he pulled the rubber stops from the bottom of the legs, then banged the frame down violently.
Ross was beginning to sweat. He also felt an uncontrollable rage constricting his chest.
He yanked one of the paintings from the wall, smashed the glass on a corner of the table, and carefully removed the print. Holding it up to the light, he searched for something he did not find.

Over forty minutes later, the room was a total shambles. Ross had single-handedly torn it apart. The only thing he had found was Vardney's expired passport.
Breathing heavily, Nicolas Ross mopped his brow with a clean linen handkerchief. He pulled on his jacket and overcoat and straightened his tie. He slipped Vardney's passport into his coat pocket, picked up his hat from the table, then left the room.
The passport was not what he had been looking for.

The new part of the School, built after GTT had purchased the property, consisted of a long, low construction of yellow brick stretching back from the original house. This housed the four labs. There were other facilities below ground. Vardney worked in Lab 10-A. This was where Hutchins was waiting for Ross. Hutchins had lighted his pipe. He was sitting on a corner of the desk in Vardney's office.
Outside the office, through the frosted glass, the other scientists seemed like ghostly blurs as they went about

THE DOUBLE-CROSS CIRCUIT 37

trying to concentrate on their work. But they all knew of Vardney's disappearance. Not much work had been done today.

As Ross entered the office, Hutchins saw that the normally dapper general-director—or G-D as he was known here, an appelation which brought chuckles from the Jewish scientists on the staff—now appeared slightly flustered.

"Is there anything missing?"

"What do you mean, Mr. Ross? That's the second time you've asked."

"Are all Vardney's papers here? Did he take anything?"

"Are you suggesting he's deliberately vanished?"

"I don't know!" Ross snapped. "That's what I'm trying to determine. Dammit, Hutchins, you're supposed to help, not get underfoot!"

Outside the office, the scientists ceased moving.

Two red spots appeared in Hutchins's veiny cheeks. In silence, he climbed from the desk. Taking out a key, he opened Vardney's desk drawers and began extracting folders which he piled on the desk top.

"There, Mr. Ross," Hutchins said icily, "you can look for yourself."

Ross opened one of the folders, held up a sheet of crabbed writing, covered with formulas and mathematical notations, and shrugged.

"I'm sorry, Hutchins, really. This . . . has come at the wrong time, that's all. You know I can't read his . . . stuff."

For the first time since Ross's arrival, Hutchins smiled.

"Neither can I," he said quietly. "I could never keep up with him."

Ross slumped into the chair and stared blankly at Hutchins. After a moment, he shook his head as though dispelling a profoundly depressing thought.

"What do you think happened to him?"

Hutchins's large hands spread open.

"I don't know. I imagine he's in a ditch or field somewhere. I'm afraid he may have hurt himself. Perhaps he's fallen and banged his head. . . ."

"So you think it's an accident?"

"Well, it looks like one, no? His . . . bouts were growing worse, they were getting longer. I know I should have been more careful. It's an awful thing to say, but I got used to them. He was so brilliant when he was sober. When you'd see him at work, you'd forgive his violence, his rages, his staggering about at four in the morning raving. . . ."

Hutchins's voice cracked; he stared out through the window at the rolling green countryside beyond.

"Let's assume," Ross began more gently, "that he is hurt somewhere, that we find him in the next few days, and that he needs hospitalization: what happens with his work? Does it come to a complete halt if he's not there? It may sound callous of me, but I have to think of his work—so much depends on it."

Hutchins turned around.

"He didn't work entirely alone, you know. Horvath and Peters were with him for the initial phases of the UNICOM design. Under his direction, they would do the 'translating'; they'd convert his thoughts into reality."

Ross's expression appeared to brighten.

"So they could read these?" He pointed to the folders on the desk.

"I imagine so. I'll have Horvath come in here."

Hutchins stood up and walked over to the door.

"On second thought, Hutchins, perhaps it's best if no one else gets involved in this," Ross said suddenly.

Hutchins hesitated, evidently awaiting some kind of

explanation. After several moments, he realized none was forthcoming. He returned to his seat.

Ross was staring out into space, frowning. While it was true that Horvath and Peters could possibly have done the modifications on the UNICOM that were necessary for the Russians to gain access, it would also have been obvious to the two scientists that an irregularity was being added to the cipher system. Ross knew he could control Vardney; Horvath and Peters, on the other hand, might have been disturbed by the moral implications. It was best if they were kept out of it altogether.

"What are you going to do?" Hutchins inquired gently. "Do you want me to notify the police?"

Ross shook his head wearily.

"No, not yet. If it comes to that, I'll notify them myself. I don't know what I am going to do, frankly. Can you remember anything unusual he said or did before disappearing?"

"I'm afraid not," Hutchins answered. "I can't even say whether he seemed more preoccupied than usual. I mean, he always appeared crushed. He was . . . He is such a strange man.

"The horrible thing, you see, is that although he was obviously an unhappy, tormented creature, we got used to it. There was Eric prowling about, always in the blackest of moods, and we never seemed to notice. Except when he'd been drinking, of course. Then, we couldn't help but notice him. Even so, we were used to Eric's temper—as though he'd become a kind of peculiar mascot that no one really took seriously any longer.

"The only time he still managed to impress was when he worked. A totally different Vardney surfaced then. He was quiet, absorbed, and so utterly brilliant.

"It's tragic. A man of such extremes. And the more arresting he was in the lab, the sorrier I felt for him."

Hutchins fell silent, shaking his head.

Ross gazed at the research director.

"I wouldn't feel overly sorry for him, Hutchins. We sit here thinking of poor drunken Vardney lying bleeding in a field and we could be wrong.

"If only I could be sure that's all that has happened to him. But I can't. Friend Vardney may have a weakness for the bottle but he's no sot. He's a little brighter than that. And precisely for that reason, I'm very much afraid Vardney has done something far worse.

"I'm afraid Vardney has defected and taken all the secrets of the UNICOM along with him!"

Within the hour, Nicolas Ross's black Rolls-Royce was racing down the M1, headed back to London. Propped against the comfortable leather upholstery, Ross glared moodily at the steady stream of traffic on the opposite side of the dual highway traveling north.

Voicing his suspicions to Hutchins had produced the desired effect. Hutchins's resistance ceased immediately. His personal feelings for Vardney became secondary. The issue was now beyond personalities. A more immediate danger—voiced by Ross—had surfaced. The Company was threatened. In the face of this, loyalty was unquestioned, almost instinctive. It never failed.

Ross left the School, assured of Hutchins's complete collaboration. But that did not help Ross solve the problem of Vardney. True, he left Bletchley Park confident there would not be further difficulties from that direction. However, he still had no idea where Vardney could have gone, nor whether Vardney had taken any of his papers with him.

Worst of all, he was beginning to fear that, unless Vardney reappeared soon, Tomas Herscu in Moscow would not be able to put forward CONSERV's offer to the Russians. For the UNICOM modifications applied to the system being installed for NATO; without the modifications, the NATO system—as contracted—would be absolutely secure and CONSERV would have lost its most important trump with the Russians.

The first question that Ross began to consider, as his gaze ceased to focus on the northbound traffic, was whether he believed the suspicion he had voiced to Jack Hutchins. Could Vardney have defected?

As Ross reflected, he realized he already knew the answer. For Ross understood Vardney much better than Hutchins did. Ross had known Vardney for over thirty years and, accordingly, was fully aware of the extent of Vardney's hatred of GTT, CONSERV, and Ross himself.

Yes, Vardney had a great many reasons to feel hatred. If he had defected, it was not for want of a motive: thirty years of accumulated spite. The reason would not have been political. Vardney was about as political as a fly. Like a great many scientists, he had very childish political views. Then again, how many defections are really political anyway?

Ross rubbed his eyebrows, then pressed his palms against his eyelids until his eyes watered.

Assuming Vardney *had* defected, the man's timing could not have been better chosen. And if the Russians now had Vardney, what did that change? This was the next question.

The answer depended on what the Russians were after. Having Vardney in their keep did not invalidate the work they wanted done from CONSERV. Eventually perhaps, but not right away. Vardney was just a brain and whereas that brain could in time create almost anything, CONSERV for a while still had the advantage of GTT's organization behind it. At best, if they had Vardney, the Russians might suddenly demand a shorter contract.

Ross made a mental note to warn Herscu of the implications of any such request on the part of the State Committee for Science and Technology.

Unless, Ross continued his line of thought, unless they wanted Vardney for a specific reason. Such as keeping him secretly hidden away but using his presence in the USSR to blackmail CONSERV into giving them *exactly what CONSERV was already prepared to give them: access into NATO.*

Now *that* would be interesting. Ross could just imagine the delicate cat-and-mouse game that would take place in Moscow, each side assuming the other knew but not saying anything outright.

Vardney's presence alone did not guarantee Soviet access into the NATO system. That required CONSERV's collaboration since CONSERV crews were already at work in NATO headquarters.

The situation was replete with ramifications. But one thing was now clear to Ross: Vardney's disappearance meant that the CONSERV negotiating team in Moscow would carry on as per the decision taken at this morning's directors' meeting. Herscu would have to watch his opponent, Chairman Gvashvili, with great care, waiting for a contra-indication.

For it was still just an assumption that Vardney had indeed gone over to the other side.

Ross reached into his coat pocket and withdrew Vardney's passport. He stared a moment at Vardney's haggard features. Then he leaned forward and slid open the mahogany panel before him. He picked up the radio-telephone receiver and dialed the mobile operator.

"Calling a London number, please . . ."

The black Rolls came into Grosvenor Square by way of North Audley Street. The huge burnished eagle on the façade of the American Embassy seemed to stare longingly into Mayfair. Inside the embassy, the neon lights were already on even though dusk was still an hour away. The Rolls drove slowly past the embassy without stopping.

The man was waiting at the corner of South Audley and Mount. The Rolls drew up and the man climbed in next to Ross. The door closed and the Rolls moved on.

"So?" the man asked.

Ross noted that he kept both hands slightly flexed on his knees. The man had short blond hair; the corners of his eyes were heavily pleated.

"A problem," Ross said and handed the man Vardney's passport. "He disappeared three days ago. Here's his expired passport. He may have requested a new one, I don't know. I can't say if he's in England still or not. Naturally, I can't go to Scotland Yard about this—they'd only ask questions about the nature of his work. That's why I called you. I need this man back; he's absolutely crucial to the outcome of negotiations we're currently having with the Russians. I'm sure your people can fill you in on anything else you may need to know."

The man put the passport in his inside breast pocket without looking at it.

"You want us to find him; and then?"

"I want him back alive and I'd like to know where he's been."

"We'll keep our eyes and ears open. I'll call you if anything comes up."

"At the office."

The man pressed the intercom switch to speak to the chauffeur.

"Oxford Circus tube station, please," he said, assuming a British accent.

As the Rolls crossed to the east side of Oxford Circus, lemminglike crowds of office workers were converging into the Underground in their nightly rush homeward.

The man turned to Ross.

"Cheerio, then."

". . . Porter," Ross murmured.

The CIA's station-chief in Britain was quickly swallowed up by the surging throngs.

It was early morning in Moscow. The black water trucks had almost finished hosing down Red Square. Against the dark green of the asphalt, the red brick of the Kremlin stood out starkly. Lenin's mausoleum had the color of dried blood.

Several bulky women in gray were sweeping.

Just to the northwest, where Gorky Street meets Marx Avenue, stands the Hotel Moskva. Inside suite 918, Tomas Herscu, exhausted by the flight back from London, was sleeping soundly when the call came through.

Tapping a telephone always drains off some of the current. That was why Nicolas Ross's voice was fainter than normal.

"I imagine I woke you?" Ross asked.

"Yes, but no matter," Herscu replied. Ross was not supposed to call.

"You're meeting with the Committee tomorrow, then?"

"That's right." Herscu frowned. Something wasn't right.

"You know the professor's report we spoke about?"

"Yes." Neither had spoken of any report.

"We won't get it; apparently it's been mislaid."

Herscu felt an unpleasant sensation in his bowel.

"In his department?"

"I don't know. He could sity. We are exploring ev

"Very absent-minded fel the report appears or v recommendations."

"No, carry on. Hopefull it's not there? Perhaps u over?"

"Ah yes; I'll ask around suitcase."

"That's it. You'll call aft

"I will."

"If you don't find it th cussed here still applies."

"I understand."

Herscu waited before h occurred shortly. The Ru pretending.

Herscu slowly stood u asleep, he had looked forwa no enthusiasm at all.

Vardney had disappeared could be in Russia.

Herscu lit a cigarette ar stared down into the street with the State Committee than he had anticipated.

Inside the hotel basemen to the incoming cables con center, the KGB men were script of Ross's conversatio the quadruplicate form, ne to," was a name:

Dr. Matv Science and tific preoce KGB.

Five

At SDECE headquarters on the boulevard Mortier, Blake found the file waiting on his desk. Attached to the file was a short note from Colonel Santerre, Blake's boss. Blake read the note. He mentally envisaged Santerre's long face, the pencil mustache and tight lips.

"Blaiykh," he mimicked Santerre's clipped speech, "drop everything else and spend the next few weeks on this one. See what you can come up with."

They all called him "Blaiykh," or "Blèk," or even "Blèkie" affectionately. No Frenchman could pronounce his name correctly. Once, he had tried to show them how it was done, but the Gallic tongue balked at the English *a*. Now he didn't care; whatever the mispronunciation, it was still better than some of the things he had been called in his life.

Blake unpinned Santerre's note, crumpled it up, and tossed it into the trash basket. He flipped through the file to see how thick it was. Briefly he gazed at the photograph, taken in the morgue, of the suicide of room 25; then he closed the file.

Before getting on with this new and most welcome assignment, he had to straighten out the files he was working on, store those that needed storing, and reassign anything current.

Blake pulled out all the files he had grown so tired of looking at and sifted through them. What a pleasure to get rid of this crap!

Student affairs: a bore, what a bore. Since May '68, when the entire French government including the special services were taken totally by surprise by the student "revolution" that came so close—if they only knew how close!—to toppling the Fifth Republic, much time, money, and manpower had been spent on "student affairs." The SDECE created a special section within R 3, Intelligence Europe, just to keep a close watch on student political life. It was Blake's misfortune to be assigned to this special section by Santerre, the boss of R 3.

Blake became very expert on the many student "*groupuscules*," and their relations with other student groups throughout Europe and America. But in the end it all became utterly boring.

There were *some* interesting finds, of course. Like the Curiel "network," created by an Egyptian-born Communist to support international student terrorism from Quebec to the heart of Africa. Yet the trail had only led to the KGB's attempting, through complicated covers, to wrest the students away from Chinese influence.

What had at first been exciting turned into routine. The information accumulated; Blake put in his hours week after week; the student movements increasingly came under the control of national secret services. The job was a *planque:* safe, comfortable, dull.

THE DOUBLE-CROSS CIRCUIT 43

The black Rolls came into Grosvenor Square by way of North Audley Street. The huge burnished eagle on the façade of the American Embassy seemed to stare longingly into Mayfair. Inside the embassy, the neon lights were already on even though dusk was still an hour away. The Rolls drove slowly past the embassy without stopping.

The man was waiting at the corner of South Audley and Mount. The Rolls drew up and the man climbed in next to Ross. The door closed and the Rolls moved on.

"So?" the man asked.

Ross noted that he kept both hands slightly flexed on his knees. The man had short blond hair; the corners of his eyes were heavily pleated.

"A problem," Ross said and handed the man Vardney's passport. "He disappeared three days ago. Here's his expired passport. He may have requested a new one, I don't know. I can't say if he's in England still or not. Naturally, I can't go to Scotland Yard about this—they'd only ask questions about the nature of his work. That's why I called you. I need this man back; he's absolutely crucial to the outcome of negotiations we're currently having with the Russians. I'm sure your people can fill you in on anything else you may need to know."

The man put the passport in his inside breast pocket without looking at it.

"You want us to find him; and then?"

"I want him back alive and I'd like to know where he's been."

"We'll keep our eyes and ears open. I'll call you if anything comes up."

"At the office."

The man pressed the intercom switch to speak to the chauffeur.

"Oxford Circus tube station, please," he said, assuming a British accent.

As the Rolls crossed to the east side of Oxford Circus, lemminglike crowds of office workers were converging into the Underground in their nightly rush homeward.

The man turned to Ross.

"Cheerio, then."

". . . Porter," Ross murmured.

The CIA's station-chief in Britain was quickly swallowed up by the surging throngs.

It was early morning in Moscow. The black water trucks had almost finished hosing down Red Square. Against the dark green of the asphalt, the red brick of the Kremlin stood out starkly. Lenin's mausoleum had the color of dried blood.

Several bulky women in gray were sweeping.

Just to the northwest, where Gorky Street meets Marx Avenue, stands the Hotel Moskva. Inside suite 918, Tomas Herscu, exhausted by the flight back from London, was sleeping soundly when the call came through.

Tapping a telephone always drains off some of the current. That was why Nicolas Ross's voice was fainter than normal.

"I imagine I woke you?" Ross asked.

"Yes, but no matter," Herscu replied. Ross was not supposed to call.

"You're meeting with the Committee tomorrow, then?"

"That's right." Herscu frowned. Something wasn't right.

"You know the professor's report we spoke about?"

"Yes." Neither had spoken of any report.

"We won't get it; apparently it's been mislaid."

Herscu felt an unpleasant sensation in his bowel.

"In his department?"

"I don't know. He could have left it at another university. We are exploring every possibility."

"Very absent-minded fellow. Should I hold on until the report appears or what? Those are important recommendations."

"No, carry on. Hopefully it'll turn up. Are you sure it's not there? Perhaps unknowingly it was brought over?"

"Ah yes; I'll ask around then. Maybe in somebody's suitcase."

"That's it. You'll call after the meeting?"

"I will."

"If you don't find it there, then the matter we discussed here still applies."

"I understand."

Herscu waited before hanging up. The telltale click occurred shortly. The Russians had long since ceased pretending.

Herscu slowly stood up. Last night, before falling asleep, he had looked forward to today. Suddenly he felt no enthusiasm at all.

Vardney had disappeared. Ross suspected the scientist could be in Russia.

Herscu lit a cigarette and, standing by the window, stared down into the street below. Tomorrow's meeting with the State Committee was going to be a lot tougher than he had anticipated.

Inside the hotel basement, in the room they had next to the incoming cables connected to the hotel switching center, the KGB men were already typing up the transcript of Ross's conversation with Herscu. At the top of the quadruplicate form, next to the heading "Attention to," was a name:

Dr. Matvei Gvashvili, Chairman, State Committee for Science and Technology, who, in addition to his scientific preoccupations, was also a major-general in the KGB.

So a change now was more than welcome. Even Saundra, Blake's lady, had seized on his lethargy to reopen discussions on the subject of "Let's Get Married." Over the last few months, Blake had watched his life settling into a pattern which was beginning to suffocate him. He didn't like the way things were going; he talked of quitting his work altogether but he did not know what else he wished to do. He waited and hoped for a change—something—anything but "student affairs."

It took Blake about twenty minutes to clear his desk, to divest himself of Marxist-Leninists, of the real honest-to-God Workers' Party, of yet another Trotskyite splinter group, and all the other Ites, Ists, and Isms that had cluttered up his mind and life for far too long. With the smile that Sisyphus might wear if finally his rock were to cease rolling back down the hill, Blake returned to his now empty desk, lit a Gitane, and flipped open the folder stamped UNSOLVED by Inspector Verrier of the Aubervilliers CID.

Blake began to read his new assignment.

Blake was a Dunkirk baby. In the course of those awful months of Summer 1940, as Guderian's Panzer divisions sliced through France and pressed the remnants of her armies and the British Expeditionary Force onto a narrow strip of beach by the sea, two lives came together amid the chaos and the screams of the Stuka dive bombers. One was a British army officer; the other a young Parisienne who had fled her city in the panic that preceded the arrival of the Germans. They met among the ragged troops, the blackened faces of the defeated, the disarmed, the wounded, and the frightened. They stayed together until he was separated from her to embark with his unit on one of the tiny boats of the makeshift armada that came from England. Civilians had to wait. She waited, a numbered tag around her neck. She was among those left behind.

Blake was born in Paris under the Occupation. A bastard. He was seven before he learned he was a bastard. Before that, everybody's father was either a prisoner or fighting far away. But the other kids' fathers came home after the war—those who hadn't "fallen in the field of Honor." Blake's father never came back. One day Blake returned from school with a bloody nose. That was the day he learned the word *bâtard*.

All he knew about his father was that he was a wonderful man and that he was in "l'intelligence service." He bore his father's name and grew up with a heroic view of his father, a view carefully nurtured by his mother. When Blake turned fifteen, his mother showed him the letter she had received in 1948, the year she learned her Blake had married an English girl during the war. She had known all along; she had brought up her son to believe his father was one of the men of the Resistance. She was in love with this man all her life. For a number of years after turning fifteen, Blake was very bitter about his father.

At eighteen, the year he was conscripted, Blake met his father for the first and only time. Without his mother's knowledge, he flew to London.

In Surbiton he found the house, a little house like all the other houses on those monotonously similar streets. There was a yellow Austin in the drive. Pink rose bushes; two empty milk bottles by the door.

His father came to the door. Did he guess when he saw the tall, brown-haired boy standing silently, trying to speak but unable to? Had he looked thus at all boys that age and wondered if one was his? Or had he completely forgotten?

Blake stared at his father, much shorter, much older, much meeker than he had ever imagined.

THE DOUBLE-CROSS CIRCUIT   51

"I'm your son," he managed eventually, and he saw the man's gray eyes change. Then Blake spat full in his father's face and ran.

Two months later, Blake was in Algeria where he stayed almost to the end of the war of independence. And often during his years there he would feel that his father's life must have been like the one he was discovering for himself.

Things repeated themselves. He was the soldier now, sent from metropolitan France to save Algeria from the FLN. And the girl he met in Algiers was half Arab as his mother had been half Jewish. And the white city was scarred with shattered buildings, barbed wire, and troops as France had been when he was born. So much was the same, yet different.

He stayed with Saundra. Then, whenever he was in Algiers; later, when it was all over and her family fled to France, he and she took an apartment in Paris.

There was just one similarity that did not appear. At first. But as the war in Algeria dragged on, as the nature of the fighting became dirtier, this too appeared. By then Blake had moved out of the conscript regiment in which he was first drafted and was now an adjutant in Massu's 10ème Division Parachutiste.

By one year, Blake had arrived too late for the battle of Algiers. The worst seemed over; the paratroops were already the heroes of the Algérois; not until the last months of the war would the FLN ever reestablish their hold on the capital. But out in the *bled*, in the areas the FLN called the *wilayas*, both sides had gone mad. A new disease carried by the virus of political warfare: *l'intox* and *contre-intox*—intoxication. Black propaganda. Secret armies. And the SDECE's notorious regiment of shock troops, the 11ème Choc.

The 11th shock regiment belongs to the secret history of the Algerian war. Its existence has never been officially recognized; the names of its officers and men are still protected behind the amnesty law passed at the end of the conflict. The "11th shock" specialized in what the French called *les coups tordus*, for which term "dirty tricks" is but a weak translation.

Blake joined the "11th shock" in late 1959. The elite regiment consisted of 300 men, grouped in three "hundreds." Some were volunteers, others conscripts with excellent records. All were drawn from the very best of the paratroop regiments.

He was sent back to France, to the regiment's secret camp at Cercottes, ten kilometers from Orléans. There, he learned how to survive and how to kill. Both courses taught him what he had not been taught in the army: that a man can survive naked in subzero temperatures, and that a man can kill another using a matchstick.

At Cercottes, Blake came into contact with the SDECE, its myths, and the men who made the myths. The *tordus*, the *dingues*—the twisted ones, the crazies. The professional soldiers who were never in uniform. The Indochina veterans, their women, their vices. They were all mad, like characters in Malraux novels, mad with courage too. Blake had never known so many Légions d'honneur among so few men.

But, back in Algeria, it wasn't quite so romantic. The "11th shock" was not there to win hearts and minds, to pacify; it operated far beyond even the spurious legality of declared war. The "11th shock" was there to kill, to maim, to destroy.

It wasn't the atrocities in general; the FLN was just as bad. It was one atrocity in particular that finally got through to Blake as he witnessed the torture of a suspected *fell*. Not even the act of torture—one became used to so much. The *gégêne*, as the electrical device—

THE DOUBLE-CROSS CIRCUIT 53

portable for field use—was called, was blackened with the sweat of terror, the straps encrusted. The *fellagha* had stopped screaming; in his mouth was someone's sock. It was then that Blake realized that the French paratrooper activating the switch looked even worse than the *fell*. He was mumbling something over and over and his eyes seemed to be popping out of their sockets. It was hard to tell who was the victim and who the torturer.

The nightmares about Algeria still recurred from time to time. And there were moments when he looked at Saundra and remembered she was half Arab. But these were fleeting. It was all the past.

The present was now and the morning had brought with it a new assignment.

Blake finished reading through the file. He put it down on the desk, open, and lit another cigarette.

The file was slim. It contained a preliminary report by Inspector Verrier, detailing the facts as he had found them: the man's arrival at La Tourmente, that he had spoken only two words—"*une chambre*," that the night clerk was unable to tell if the man had an accent, that the night clerk heard nothing, the discovery of the body on the following morning, and so on. There was the medical examiner's report and his findings. The two lab reports. And two photographs: one of the man as he was found kneeling by the bed in room 25, the other, face and torso, taken in the autopsy room. There was also the piece of paper on which the man had written the word UNICOM, surrounded by a series of shaky lines.

Only two items interested Blake—the photograph of the man's face and the piece of paper. The rest was the usual police paraphernalia, simultaneously useful and useless in the sense that while the information there was good to know, it didn't tell Blake very much.

He picked up the photograph and stared at it a long time. Those who die violently always look as though they have just awakened from a profound sleep. Their faces appear puffy. But there is always that air of surprise, a kind of dim perception of Finality.

The dead look stupid.

But this man's actions were calculated. He had taken great care to remove all signs of his identity beforehand. He had used a revolver so common as to be untraceable. He had established the conditions of his death in total anonymity.

Then he had left a message.

Why?

The two were contradictory.

Had he intended to eliminate himself, leaving behind an unidentifiable derelict, and then changed his mind at the last minute? Or was it all as he had planned it?

There were two emotions here, working against each other. The first was an extreme self-hatred. All indications pointed to that: a man sunk to the bottom of his anguish whose last act is to destroy the cause of his misery, himself. Then there was the complete opposite. The word UNICOM which he deliberately left behind. And this he considered important, more important than himself. This word was the signature to the man's self-portrait of his death. As though he were saying that the word UNICOM had killed him.

That was all very good except for one thing. The man was drunk! According to the medical report, there was enough alcohol in his system for him to be very drunk. But then he was an alcoholic, so had the alcohol affected him?

In other words, was he aware of his actions? Were they sequential? Logical? Had he intended to kill himself in the hotel room or was he still only contemplating it?

Blake frowned, stubbed out one cigarette and lit another.

The fact was that the man *had* killed himself. No one

could have entered after the night clerk locked the door again. And as the man in room 25 had committed suicide, this act was consistent with the circumstantial evidence of intent. Whatever his last-minute hesitations or fears, he had carried it out exactly as he apparently wanted it to be done.

"It *is* logical," Blake murmured emphatically.

He reached for the first photograph and held it up, next to the second. The dead man's kneeling position suddenly struck Blake.

Blake looked up.

If he was going to kill himself with a pistol, how would he do it?

Blake counted his ribs until he could feel the pulsations of his heart. He'd shoot into his heart, not in the mouth. There was something obscene, not to say frightfully messy, about shooting oneself in the head.

More self-hatred.

Blake also realized, to the extent one can think dispassionately about the question, that he would shoot himself seated in a chair. For the man to have shot himself on his knees, it was as though he were praying. As though the act were against his religious principles, yet he was doing it anyway because his reasons were greater.

Blake slid open one of the drawers of his desk and took out a sheet of paper. He drew a line down the middle; on one side he wrote "man," on the other "Unicom."

Under the "man" heading, he drew another line. Below this, he wrote "Catholic" followed by a question mark, then "alcoholic," a dash, and the notation "Paris clinics." At the bottom of the column, he wrote a brief psychological profile of his subject.

Now Blake tacked the two photographs to the wall that faced his desk.

He sat down and picked up the piece of paper on

which the man had written the word UNICOM. Blake slowly turned the paper around, trying to make sense of the spidery lines.

They formed a sort of weak Rorschach blot. The lines ran jaggedly up and down, curving slightly. There were more lines cutting across the top, forming a large, trembling lower-case *t*. In from the shape, to the right, was a dot. There were more dots at the bottom of the sheet. And three drops of blood.

Blake turned the sheet this way and that, but the lines told him nothing.

Taking a separate sheet of paper from his desk, he wrote UNICOM across the top. Then COMUNI.

At once Blake knew why Santerre had given him the file. Santerre was reflecting the government's ever-present nightmare that the Left would overcome its divisiveness and form a United Front that could topple the Gaullist coalitions.

For a moment Blake considered the possibility. Could UNICOM be the name of a future Communist International? Then why the man's suicide? Had there ever been a suicide among the opposition parties as a result of factional disputes? Unlikely.

No, this line of thought made little sense. There were too many SDECE agents among the major opposition parties for a significant policy change of this sort not to be known.

Unless UNICOM stood for a political grouping among the immigrants. . . .

Under the "Unicom" heading, Blake wrote "political party?" Suddenly he felt listless. If this is what it was, it would be no different from "student affairs."

Blake looked up and stared at the face of the dead man. Strangely, he felt a sense of empathy toward this figure with no identity. There was something in the man's face that Blake had seen before.

Blake leaned forward, resting his hands beneath his chin.

"Who are you?" he murmured.

There was no response, of course. The dead man's eyes continued to stare upward.

Now Blake understood what the man's expression reminded him of. It was the same transfigured look found in quattrocento paintings of the Church Saints—the rapturous face of exaltation.

The longer Blake gazed at the man's photograph, the more certain he became that this affair was not the result of some émigré squabble.

The man had died a martyr, but to what? Blake had no idea, but he did know he wanted to find the answer. He drew his telephone toward him, and dialed two digits.

"*Salut*, Cerbère, it's Blake. I'm coming down."

If anyone could help him, Cerbère was the one. Cerbère knew everything.

Six

Tomas Herscu let his gaze run slowly around the room. A thousand reflections flashed from the huge crystal chandelier. The domed ceiling vaulted upward, cavernous like a cathedral's. Around the long rectangular tables covered with green felt, the two negotiating teams faced each other, like ministers about to sign a treaty.

Why here? Herscu wondered, and why today?

The fleet of black Zils had arrived at the usual time. But instead of taking the CONSERV people to the Ministry of Foreign Trade where the negotiations had always previously been held, the convoy raced inside the Kremlin walls and stopped before the imposing nineteenth century façade of the Bolshoi Kremlyovsky Palace.

In the Soviet Union, nothing occurs by accident. All is meticulously planned. The Russians tend to make you forget this, with their rude manners, ill-cut clothes, and sleepy expressions. That too is calculated; it creates a

THE DOUBLE-CROSS CIRCUIT

false sense of confidence; you end up believing you are dealing with bumpkins. It is all false. Everything in Russia is a mirage and you are the pawn on the world's largest chessboard.

So why, Herscu asked himself, have they suddenly decided to show us such solicitude? Treating us as they would a government delegation, and not just any government but one in whose policies they recognize their self-interest? The answer, Herscu knew, rested only with one man present.

Herscu lowered his eyes and stared across the table.

As usual, Matvei Gvashvili's face appeared vacant. His huge head sprouted out of his vast shoulders. He wore the rumpled black suit he always wore, the too-tight jacket buttoned even though he was seated.

A great showman, Gvashvili. He behaved like a trained bear; he fell asleep during the discussions—once he had begun snoring loudly. When he was awake, he roared and bellowed, pounding the table with his large hairless hands, and leaping to his feet as though his three hundred pounds were nothing. It was all show.

Behind the small gray eyes sat a razor-sharp mind. Not just as a scientist—Gvashvili was a member of the Akademiia Naouka SSSR, the Soviet Academy of Science, appointed for his work in astrophysics—but in every respect. As a negotiator. As a politician. Gvashvili was a Georgian like Stalin. Like the dead dictator, he could be utterly ruthless and he could be completely charming; not for a second did he ever forget what he was after.

Herscu had seen Stalin only once—in 1951. Gvashvili was a larger version, the mustache was the same, the honey-brown hair too. Herscu had often wondered whether Gvashvili flaunted the resemblance deliberately. It was a measure of his power that he could get away with it.

Gvashvili's plump yellow fingers toyed with the blue

cover of the folder in front of him. He saw that Herscu was looking at him.

Gvashvili opened the folder and reread the typescript of Nicolas Ross's conversation with Herscu the day before. The words "professor's report," "mislaid," and "over there" had been heavily circled in blue. The conversation only confirmed what Gvashvili had already guessed at: CONSERV wanted something more than the contract. It had to be. Because of something that happened twenty-five years ago.

But what could CONSERV be after now?

For weeks, Gvashvili had been waiting patiently for Herscu to indicate what this could be. The Rumanian had not shown his hand. Gvashvili felt a certain admiration for Herscu who hid his hatred of the Russians extremely well. Gvashvili knew that Herscu had not had a pleasant time of it in the Lubyanka in 1951. Gvashvili continued to wait.

Three days ago, Herscu was called back to London. Now Gvashvili knew "it" would be imminent. The telephone conversation made him certain. Through that poorly coded conversation, Ross had told Gvashvili as much. There was no doubt in Gvashvili's mind that Ross *wanted* him to know CONSERV was after something more.

It was thoughtful of Ross to have reminded Gvashvili in this way. But there was no need. Even after twenty-five years, Gvashvili had not forgotten.

It was a variation of the law that says a criminal always returns to the scene of the crime. Especially when the "crime" had failed the first time.

Gvashvili suddenly closed the folder. The Committee member who had been rambling on all this while saw the chairman's gesture and rapidly ended his remarks.

Gvashvili leaned toward the microphone.

"*Gospoda*," he said, his voice booming through the

chamber, "gentlemen, we break for tea and coffee a half-hour."

Against background sounds of rattling cups and saucers, Matvei Gvashvili made his way across the room toward Herscu. The Rumanian watched the Russian approach. Gvashvili, a full head taller than anyone else, paused here and there to exchange a few words, to smile, to pat someone on the back.

The time has come, Herscu reflected fatalistically.

Earlier, he had realized why the meeting today was taking place here: a direct result of the call from Ross. Herscu knew the Russians had been listening in. Once again they were showing interest in the outcome of the negotiations. Or was it that, having Vardney safely in the USSR, they now wanted to discuss whatever the scientist might have told them?

Herscu took a sip of coffee. He could not shake an unpleasant sensation of reliving his past. He did not like it.

Suddenly the chairman was beside him.

Gvashvili reached for a cup and filled it from the silver samovar on the table. He turned to Herscu.

"Mr. Herscu," Gvashvili began affably, "I've been told you lost a report of some kind. I trust you've been able to locate it?"

"You're very well informed, Mr. Chairman. As a matter of fact, I haven't found it yet."

The two men peered at each other over the lips of their cups.

"Let's get away from the crowd," Gvashvili offered, gesturing Herscu toward a corner of the room.

"It's very annoying," Herscu said a moment later when the two stood a little to the side, "for this is a most valuable report. It pertains to a system we've designed for one of our clients."

"I see," Gvashvili said, his voice commiserative, "may I ask which one, if this is not overstepping the limits of confidence?"

"Not at all; I'm sure you already know about our work for the North Atlantic Treaty Organization."

"NATO? I wasn't aware. What sort of system is it?"

Watching Gvashvili, Herscu abruptly realized Vardney was *not* in Russia.

"A completely new communications security system. Absolutely impenetrable. We're very proud of it."

Gvashvili's gray eyes did not move from Herscu's face.

"And a report explaining how this system works has been mislaid? How very annoying."

"Yes, very," Herscu said, draining his cup. Now he was certain. They did *not* have Vardney.

"When something has been lost, assistance in searching for it is always useful, is it not?"

"Assuredly, Mr. Chairman. We were contemplating an appeal for assistance, and a reward."

"That's very generous of you. We are a generous people also."

"I am glad to hear you say that, Mr. Chairman. We have always been aware of the generosity of the Russian people. It is so regrettable that politics for too long stood in the way of mutual understanding and collaboration."

"I fully share your regrets. Fortunately, misunderstandings are things of the past today."

"It would certainly appear to be the case. I for one am more than hopeful as to the imminent and satisfactory conclusion of our discussions."

"Any way in which we can assist one another is naturally an important step in that direction. Yes, I too see an agreement arrived at quite soon. However, you

THE DOUBLE-CROSS CIRCUIT 63

must first locate that which is lost. I gather there is some question as to its being here, in this country?"

"You may be right. I'm such a disorganized person. I'll just have to look among my things more carefully. All those suitcases! You know, I wouldn't be surprised if it were in my hotel room."

Gvashvili too emptied his cup.

"Yes, when one travels one often takes more luggage than is needed."

"That's exactly it! I knew I needn't have brought the small gray suitcase."

Gvashvili shrugged.

"There you go. You see, it's always worthwhile to discuss these things with friends. Excuse me, Mr. Herscu, there's someone I wish to talk to. It's been most interesting."

Gvashvili put down his cup and hurried over to one of the Committee members.

Herscu returned to his place on the CONSERV side of the negotiating tables.

He knew that when he reentered his hotel suite later that evening one of his suitcases would have disappeared. The small gray one that contained copies of the blueprints of the NATO UNICOM system, brought back by Herscu after the London meeting with the other directors.

He wondered how long it would take the Russians to determine that, without CONSERV's collaboration, the plans themselves were useless.

Shortly after six, Tomas Herscu stepped out of the elevator on the ninth floor of the Hotel Moskva. He got his key from the floor clerk, a sallow-faced woman looking very unhappy perched on her stool behind the wooden desk.

Herscu walked down the ill-lit corridor to suite 918. Unlocking the door, he stood a moment in the doorway. The rank odor of Russian tobacco still hovered in the room.

"Subtle lot," Herscu murmured and snapped on the light.

Sure enough, the small gray suitcase was gone. A *papirossa* had been left in one of the ashtrays.

Though he knew they had been in his room—at his invitation—he nonetheless felt violated. It reminded him how far away he was, how completely at their mercy. . . .

A wave of depression shook Herscu.

He moved to the dresser, pulled open the top left drawer, and pulled out the bottle of J&B whiskey. He held it up to the light to make certain they had not drunk any.

They had. The level in the bottle had dropped a quarter-inch.

"Bloody swine," Herscu swore.

He contemplated pouring the contents into the toilet, then changed his mind. After carefully wiping the neck, he took a long swig.

It helped a little.

He had not removed his coat.

One by one, he examined the locks of the other suitcases. There were no scratches.

With his foot he slid the black Samsonite suitcase toward the center of the room. It took him a minute to dial the three combination locks. Inside this suitcase was another one, identical in shape but smaller. It too had three combination locks. And two additional locks in the rear hinges which he opened with a special key.

The suitcase contained a laser telephone set complete with miniaturized transmitter. It was a working model of a system whose bugs were still being ironed out at the

THE DOUBLE-CROSS CIRCUIT 65

School in Bletchley Park. This had only one frequency and could send but not receive. Yet it was powerful enough to beam to England, and it possessed the great advantage of not needing to pass through the Soviet phone system.

First, Herscu took out a small plastic box. He screwed the short tripod legs into the base and set the thing down on the floor.

This was a precaution as it was likely the room was bugged. When on, the device emitted regular pulsations at a frequency low enough to turn a microphone's reception into steady static—as though the person being listened in upon were using an electric razor.

Herscu got up and locked the door.

As he sat down again, he switched on the interference device. Simultaneously he activated the laser phone. All he had to do was wait for the red light beside the voice unit to come on.

Over one thousand miles to the west, the signal would be picked up by a special disk antenna atop Centre Place in London. The Russians would not notice a thing. The laser phone's frequency was much too high. After all, it was precisely because of Western technological superiority in such matters that CONSERV had come to Moscow.

The red light appeared and Herscu pressed the button that would convert the sound of his voice into light signals.

"London, this is Fortress Blue." As in radio, there was a call sign which told the listener whether the call was voluntary or whether Herscu was being forced to make it. Had he said "Fortress Red," Ross would have known that Herscu was calling under duress.

"The offer has been made and delivery accepted. It will require a little time for them to examine contents and realize they need us in order to proceed further.

"The advance was made very directly by counterpart who give a literal interpretation of your call to me. The material I had brought became 'the professor's report.' I responded on that basis.

"Counterpart showed no indication of awareness that it is not the report but the professor who has been mislaid. Has he been located by the way?

"I do not like the overall direction. If the professor does not return, we are headed for a repeat of Sandstone. Once again, we will be offering more than we can deliver. They will not appreciate it a second time.

"If that is what you are intending, for God's sake take me out of here beforehand. I do not want to find myself in those cells again. Do you understand me?

"After they have examined material, I will resume private discussion with counterpart. Will report then.

"In the meantime, find the professor!

"Fortress Blue ending now."

On the eighteenth floor of Centre Place, Nicolas Ross stared at the receiver built into the wall of his office. He heard Herscu terminate; there was a piercing sputter of static, then silence.

Considering the signal had to travel unamplified until West Germany before it could be picked up and boosted through GTT amplifiers, the laser phone worked remarkably well.

Ross stood up from behind his desk and went over to the window. Pursing his lips, he stared outward.

What else could he do for the moment?

Wait. Hope that Herscu lasted despite the tension. Trust that the CIA located Vardney in time.

Wait ... hope ... trust ...

These were not conditions in which Ross liked to work. All his life he had counted on conditions other than these to see him through. Now he was impotent to do other but wait, hope and trust.

Nor did he need Herscu reminding him of Operation Sandstone!

The name alone sent shivers of frustration through Ross. Sandstone, his only failure, the first time Vardney had crossed him. He had still trusted Vardney then. It had never occurred to him that because of Vardney three people would die by firing squad in Russia and young Herscu would see the torture chambers of the Lubyanka Prison in Moscow.

But Vardney *had* crossed him; the three *were* shot and Herscu narrowly missed a similar fate. Because of Vardney, Sandstone had failed.

And for twenty-five years, Ross was forced to steer away from Russia and the Russian markets until the bad blood subsided.

Twenty-five years and how many millions of dollars had Vardney cost him! And now Vardney once again threatened to jeopardize Ross's crowning achievement.

Nicolas Ross stared at London below him, stretching endlessly toward the four horizons.

Somewhere out there, among the ants that he could see crawling about their business, was Vardney.

Wait ... hope ... trust ...

He had no choice.

If the going became too hard for Herscu, he'd fly to Moscow and deal with Gvashvili in person. This time the Russian contract would go through—Vardney or no Vardney. It had to.

Nicolas Ross turned away from the window. His eyes fell upon the telephones on his desk.

What the hell was the CIA doing? Why hadn't they located him yet?

Just over a mile from Centre Place, Porter was in his office on the top floor of the American Embassy in Grosvenor Square.

He looked at his watch and calculated that it was morning in the United States. Reaching for the telephone he kept locked inside the drawer of his desk, he dialed the direct number that connected him to the headquarters of the Central Intelligence Agency in Langley, Virginia, eight miles from downtown Washington.

"Hello, Riverside, this is Soho. . . . Is there anything new on that man I inquired about? . . . Vardney, Eric H., that's the one. . . . I'll wait. . . . I'm still there. . . . He requested and received a new passport two months ago? Not through this embassy. . . . I see. He applied directly but it was sent to him through the embassy here. Very well, give me the number and dates of issue. . . ." Porter reached for a pencil and jotted down the numbers on a yellow legal pad by the phone.

"I got those. Any visas or permissions to travel in the Curtain countries? . . . Nothing? . . . Anything else? . . . Well, keep on it. I want all stations alerted about this. In fact, upgrade the priority. . . . That'll do fine. If there's anything, the slightest request concerning Vardney or UNICOM from anywhere, I want to know about it immediately, day or night.

"Thanks, Riverside. Soho out."

Porter replaced the receiver in its cradle. There was nothing to do but keep waiting. It was like that. You waited and waited. Until you got lucky.

Seven

THE MAN walked into the hotel room and carefully locked the door. On the bed he placed his small cheap suitcase. Smiling, he sat at the desk. He opened one of the drawers, found a sheet of paper inside and with the pen which he unclipped from his breast pocket quickly wrote out a word. He was laughing to himself as he returned to the bed and snapped open the suitcase. He was still laughing as he slowly knelt down on the floor. Tears streamed down his gaunt cheeks; his mouth opened wide; his finger squeezed hard. The explosion echoed ... echoed ... echoed ...

With a cry, Blake awoke. He sat upright, kicking the sheet from his body. The sound of the shot continued to reverberate in his mind.

Blake leaned over and turned on the lamp beside the bed. The sight of his own apartment and its familiar contents gradually dispelled the sense of horror left by the nightmare.

Saundra had her back to him. Her long hair, henna-red like the soil of Algeria, grew down to her hips, forming a train that fanned out on the sheets. She slept curled up, her hands tucked between her thighs.

Blake reached for his cigarettes. His wrist watch on the night table showed four o'clock. He lit a cigarette and began to cough.

Saundra stirred.

"Are you awake?" she groaned, her voice childishly plaintive.

Blake grunted.

Saundra sighed and turned toward him. Sleep made her cheekbones seem even higher. Her green eyes, normally large, were narrow slits.

"Your cigarette stinks," she complained.

Blake did not reply. He looked at her vaguely, indifferent to her nakedness. After a moment her eyes opened further.

"Why are you awake?" she asked softly, reaching out to place a hand on his thigh.

"I was dreaming about my suicide."

"Your own? Sounds thrilling."

"Not my own. The man in the hotel room."

"Oh, him. Can't you leave all that where it belongs?"

Saundra did not know about the SDECE. As far as she was concerned Blake was "in the police." The particulars didn't interest her. In part because after the brutality she had witnessed in her homeland she did not want to be told any more than the minimum. But there was something else, a characteristically French trait which North American women have never been able to grasp. Saundra was with her man, not his job. Blake's work was something he did. That was all.

"No, it bothers me. I have the feeling I see only the end result of a long process whose development I can't grasp. I'm being challenged to understand and I'm not succeeding."

She closed her eyes.

"You men and your challenges. The light's hurting my eyes."

Blake turned off the light. He continued to smoke in the darkness.

"You'll get back to it in the morning," she said. "Come and sleep. If you want a challenge, here's one."

He felt her fingers move along his thigh. Blake put out his cigarette and lay back on the bed, enjoying what she was doing. His body responded to her touch, like a slug in thoughtless contentment at being alive. But Blake's mind went on worrying about a man who had chosen to die.

"Sorry, Blake," said Cerbère with the tone of a doctor announcing a patient's demise. After Blake's call the day before, Cerbère had diligently gone to work on his beloved computers, researching possible sources of information that could produce an identity to the suicide in the hotel room. To no avail.

Cerbère's real name was Pierre Le Quoélleq, but no one ever called him that. He was known as Cerbère because the name was similar to the machines whose guardian he was.

The machines—specifically two banks of Honeywell-Bull-CII computers—were named CYBER, a contraction of *cybernétique*. He was Cerbère. It was simple, straightforward, and clear.

It was also appropriate. For one, because Cerbère, who was short and perpetually frowning, resembled a bulldog and so had a physical similarity to the mythical Cerberus even if he did not have the original's many heads. For another, the SDECE's Cerbère was in a very real sense the guardian of the secrets of Hell.

Of all the Western democracies, France comes closest to being a police state. Not just because of the numerous police forces, paramilitary police, army, and secret police, but even more because of the unrelenting interest which the State shows in the doings of its citizens. From cradle to grave, there are few activities of the ordinary Frenchman which escape the attention of the State. Nor does it need pointing out that the State is constantly devising new techniques to find out more about those whose servant it supposedly is.

It all amounts to a fantastic accumulation of information. Until recently, however, the sheer volume was just too much for an archaic bureaucracy to handle. Each ministry did its own filing of information and there was neither the manpower nor the means for all the data to be centralized.

Then de Gaulle decided that France needed a computer industry of its own.

One result, among many, was that the SDECE now had access to the most complete and recent data concerning millions of lives. The best system in France. In addition to its own already considerable files, the SDECE could at the touch of a button cross-reference with the files of the Ministère des Armées, of l'Intérieur, of the PJ, of the Direction de la Surveillance du Territoire, and of the Reseignements Généraux.

It was from this gold mine that Blake hoped to extract some piece of information about his mysterious suicide.

Cerbère's "Sorry Blake" had just dashed that hope.

Blake had entered Cerbère's domain trying hard to stifle his excitement. Now he sat down heavily at the stainless steel table which Cerbère used as a desk. Around the two men, the banks of computers hummed steadily.

Cerbère, in his white lab coat, thrust his hands into his pockets.

"If it's any consolation, your man is definitely not French. Nor did he ever reside here, commit a crime, or serve in any of the colonial regiments. He's not a known or suspected agent either for us or for any foreign power operating in France.

"On the other hand, he could have at some point been here as a tourist or on a visit. But without a name I can't find out.

"It's the same story with UNICOM. I can only tell you what it is *not*. It's not a code. It's not the name of any computer we know about. Nor is it a political group or party. It's not a company or firm. And if it's a device of some sort, it's never been patented or sold in France.

"That's about it, *mon vieux*. Or rather, that's what it isn't."

Cerbère offered Blake a pitiful smile.

Blake scratched at the metal tabletop with a fingernail.

"What makes you so sure the man's not French? Nor is UNICOM, I suppose?"

"Nothing makes me *so* sure, just 95 percent sure. For one, there's not a face bearing a French passport that resembles your man. For another, if either were French there would be a trace somewhere. Of this, as I said, I can be 95 percent certain. There's always that tiny portion that sneaks through, but you have to think what that could be. I can't."

Blake looked up.

"Any suggestions?"

Cerbère shrugged.

"I don't know. Try outside. Ask the *Amerloques*. They have facilities that make ours look like a kid's toy. But if they draw a blank, you might as well forget it because this fellow of yours is a ghost."

Blake returned upstairs, brooding. Cerbère's description of the man as a ghost annoyed him. Because it was true. But the man had been alive once. It just was not possible to vanish from the face of the earth. Or was it?

There had to be a reason. An extraordinary reason.

Along the way, Blake dropped into his section of R 3 to see if there were any word on the inquiries being made by SDECE agents at the private anti-alcoholism clinics around Paris and in the south of France. It came as no surprise that there was nothing yet.

Over Blake's desk, the photograph of the dead man reflected the light streaming in from outside. Blake stood by the desk and did not sit down. He stared at the photograph as though he expected it to speak to him.

Blake abruptly turned away.

In the corridor he met Colonel Santerre, hurrying off to a meeting with a pile of dossiers under his arm.

"So Blake, anything?" The colonel's little mustache quivered.

"We have nothing. I'm going to try outside."

"Very well, but make it routine. We don't want anyone stirred up. Cheer up, lad, you're looking suicidal."

Santerre continued down the hall, his brown shoes squeaking slightly.

Blake did not try to keep up with him. In face, he came to a complete stop.

That was the third time. First Saundra thought he had dreamed of his own suicide, then Cerbère had insinuated the man did not exist, and now Santerre's remark.

The Communications Room was on the third floor. Here, through a system of relays to avoid detection from source, SDECE received radio signals from its agents abroad. Through here passed SDECE communications traffic throughout France. To the left was the electronic surveillance section with large master tapes slowly unwinding. International traffic was to the right, at the end of a short corridor.

For certain kinds of information, there exists a fair amount of intercommunication between secret services. The traffic is nowhere near the scale of an organization like Interpol and the reason for this is simple. The regular police have a common enemy in Crime; it is therefore to their advantage to collaborate as closely as possible whenever they can. This is not the case for the secret services. Here, everyone is a foe; even one's supposed allies. There are only degrees of more or less hostile.

"*Salut, petit,*" Blake said to the wavy-haired technician who was neither short nor much younger than Blake himself. "I want to send out a Routine/For Background Information to our worthy colleagues in England, Italy, Germany, and the USA."

The technician took out a form on which he began making check marks.

"Civilian or military?"

"Civilian all."

"Priority?"

"Routine, I said."

"Code?"

"Standard."

"Satellite or cable?"

"Cable."

"O.K." The technician handed Blake a metal clipboard. "Write your message in the appropiate place. Print. Don't forget to sign all the copies and put your section number. You people always leave out your numbers."

Blake returned shortly and handed back the clipboard.

The technician read in a toneless voice: "Copy SIS, Cheltenham: Copy SID, Rome; Copy BfV, Bonn; Copy

CIA, Langley. Message: Appreciate assistance identification stop UNICOM stop Any information on UNICOM would be of great value for completion SDECE investigation stop. Signed: Blake, R 3, SDECE, Paris. That's what you want sent?"

Blake nodded.

"It'll go out immediately. Responses will be sent to your section. That's why we need your section number."

Blake went back downstairs to his desk. All he could do now was wait.

The light was no longer on the photograph. The dead man's eyes stared vacantly upward.

Saundra Letellier was waiting for Blake in the English pub on la rue Mouffetard. She wore brown leather boots, knee-high, a plaid skirt, and a sheepskin jacket from Afghanistan.

Her long reddish-brown hair fell about her shoulders. She had extremely large emerald green eyes whose color contrasted strikingly with her faintly olive skin.

She too had suffered because of the war of liberation of her homeland. In many ways more than Blake, for in her the damage was psychic. It had been hard enough as a child to overcome the stigma of being half Arab, of being called a *métèque*, a half-breed, when all she wanted was to be considered *Française* like all the other children. And later, having to choose on which side her allegiance lay, a choice made so much harder in that she could understand both sides.

If she now seemed selfish, at times totally oblivious to the world beyond Blake and herself, that was as a result of the choice she came to make. For her, nothing beyond the tiny universe in which she felt at home had any importance any longer. Everything else had been either taken from her or rejected by her.

Her childhood and adolescence was a closed book to which she never returned. Gone forever was the white city of Algiers, its boulevards and its palm trees and the perpetually blue sky. Gone were the dreams she had once held of a career teaching philosophy.

She lived through the war and survived physically intact. That was more than so many of her friends had done—those who were blown apart by the *stroungas*, OAS's plastic explosives, crippled or blinded.

She had met Blake when she was still a student and he a young soldier on leave in Algiers. Blake was her link to her past and though they never talked about those days, his presence kept her from feeling totally lost. Her parents now lived in Marseilles, but she rarely saw them.

She never completed her *agrégation* in philosophy. In the context of the war, the pursuit of Truth was just too absurd.

Since the end, since the panic-stricken flight from Algiers, when she left Algeria with her parents, she had worked as a model for a while, had had a few small roles in films. But as she no longer cared about anything it had not lasted. Her indifference only aggravated the directors she worked with; she had not kowtowed to their self-importance.

For the last five years, she had worked teaching French to American executives in Paris. She did her job well and mechanically. It made no demands of her. The Americans, all charm and flattery, were kept busy thinking up new tactics that might land her in bed with them. They were still trying.

At the flat where she and Blake lived, she spent her time painting. The walls were hung with many striking canvases. Once Blake, hoping to please her, had arranged with a friend who owned a gallery for Saundra to hold an exposition. She had been furious. "The paintings are proof of my liberty," she had screamed, "and that is not for sale to anyone!" Blake had not tried again.

But Saundra had not buried all her dreams. She clung to one: that Blake would eventually stop tilting at windmills. She wanted a child. It pained her that he seemed in no hurry to share that dream with her.

She was thirty now. Recently she had decided that, unless Blake made up his mind in the course of the next year, she would leave him.

Saundra lit a Marlboro and asked the waiter for another *demi*.

Seated at the bar, a man kept turning around to leer at her. She gazed over his head, looking at the wall decorated with automobile license plates from Québec.

Blake strolled in with a faraway glaze in his eyes. His shirt collar was protruding onto the lapel of his jacket. Today's *Le Monde* poked out of his side pocket.

She knew right away what kind of day he'd had. His brown hair was standing up and he needed to shave again.

"I wish to hell that when you meet me you'd straighten yourself out a bit," she snapped. "You look like an overfull ashtray."

He chucked her under the chin and sat down opposite her, his eyes roving about the bar.

"No progress?" she asked, leaning forward to kiss him on the nose.

He stared at her and appeared ready to embark on a diatribe, then thought better of it. He took her hand.

"I've got an idea. Let's go out for dinner, have a few drinks, relax. Later, we can go home and have a long shower together, then make passionate love until dawn. O.K.?" He kissed the palm of her hand.

Her eyes seemed to grow brighter.

Several hours later, the two of them lurched drunkenly out of a small Provençal restaurant on la rue Erasme. They were holding each other around the shoulders and giggling.

"What was the name of that place?" Blake mumbled, turning on the sidewalk to see the sign. "They ought to wash the windows. Can't see a damn thing. Damn good place, damn good food, excellent wines."

He began to shout at passers-by: "Hey! Go in there. I recommend it. It's five-star!"

Huddled close to him, Saundra snickered. Her mouth felt warm against his chest.

The two marched jaggedly up the hill, loudly singing "l'Internationale."

"Debout les lamnés de la terre, debout les forçats du travail . . ."

In Rome, in Bonn, and at the British government's intelligence complex at Cheltenham, the reactions to Blake's query were pretty much the same. Shrugs, raised eyebrows. The responses were formulated. Sorry. Nothing, nothing, nothing.

But at the Central Intelligence Agency's headquarters outside Washington, things were different. There was running in the corridors. Whispered confabulations. Hurried conferences. A telephone call in the middle of the night to the man whose code name was Riverside.

Within an hour of the cable's arrival, Riverside's limousine raced through the main gates and moments later Riverside was seen, his face still puffy with sleep, walking rapidly toward his office, flanked by two nervous advisers.

---

80   *Michael Dorland*

In London, it was shortly after dawn. A feeble light dripped in through the windows of Nicolas Ross's house in Jermyn Street. Gray shadows seemed to be chasing each other.

Ever since his divorce in 1950, Ross had lived alone. He preferred it this way. His true marriage was to CONSERV and the company was more exacting than the most demanding of wives ... or mistresses.

Next to Nicolas Ross's bed, the telephone buzzed stridently. Ross surfaced from a profound slumber and groggily reached for the receiver.

"Hello," he croaked.

As soon as he recognized the voice on the other end, he was instantly awake.

"Yes, Porter, you've heard? ... There's been a request from the SDECE concerning UNICOM? ... Porter, nobody in the world could know about UNICOM unless Vardney told them. That means he's talking. You've got to get him back here! ... Look, I don't care how you go about it, just have him returned. ... I needn't remind you what's at stake. Your people said they'd collaborate if requested. I'm asking for that collaboration now, Porter! I wouldn't have come to you otherwise. ... Just get him back! ... Very well. Goodbye."

Ross hung up and fell back onto the pillows. After a moment he smiled.

They'd located Vardney. Now everything would be all right.

Eight

"Allow me to give you a lift back to your hotel, Mr. Herscu." It was not an offer. Gvashvili's tone made it a command.

Tomas Herscu uttered a few brief words to Ray Hendersley of the CONSERV negotiating team, then joined the Russian. Gvashvili was wearing a stiff beige mackintosh and an old-fashioned homburg.

The two men set off down the brightly lit corridor. On either side, guards stood at rigid attention in their parade uniforms with blue jackets and red epaulettes.

Gvashvili did not speak until the two were settled in the rear of the large black Zil. Herscu could not see out. Gray curtains covered all the windows, including the driver's partition.

"Well, Mr. Herscu," Gvashvili began, patting Herscu on the leg which made the Rumanian start. "We have examined your documents and find the UNICOM system most interesting. Most interesting.

"Regrettably so, I am afraid. As you may be aware, it was one of NATO's saving graces—for us—that the alliance did not possess a centralized communications system. This made it considerably easier for us to intercept their communications. So I must congratulate you on your progress and thank you for bringing UNICOM to our attention. Otherwise, our difficulties would shortly be increased many-fold."

Gvashvili turned toward Herscu and gave him a long look.

"My experts tell me that it is not sufficient just to duplicate the UNICOM system here in the Soviet Union. For it to have any value, a special part has to be installed in the heart of the NATO system. Only then will we be able to intercept their communications once UNICOM becomes operational. You are aware of this?"

"Yes, Mr. Chairman," Herscu said gently.

"I see. Your gift comes attached with strings. No, no, do not object. I realize this is only 'good business,' as you people say. But I had hoped there would be more evidence of trust."

"Mr. Chairman, we are not fools. It is a simple matter of guarantees."

"As you say, guarantees. Against what, I wonder? That we will not honor our contract with you? Mr. Herscu, these decisions to engage in trade with the West are not arrived at lightly, I assure you.

"And since we are speaking of guarantees, where are ours? If we accept your conditions, we become very dependent on you, do we not? At least when we use our own agents, we have some degree of control. You ask that we trust you in this. I ask 'why?' when you are not prepared to trust us?"

"Mr. Chairman, let us not mince words. To put it bluntly, we are prepared to engage in espionage on your behalf. I hardly call such a gesture one lacking in trust."

THE DOUBLE-CROSS CIRCUIT 83

"And that is what puzzles me, Mr. Herscu. You are, as you say, offering to spy for us. Why? Is it solely a matter of profit?"

"To a very large degree, yes. But it is also a question of common interest. We have everything to gain from normal peaceful endeavors between ourselves and your country. Unlike the politicians, we are not beholden to an electorate, only to our shareholders. We have a flexibility that nations cannot afford to have. To the extent that the Soviet government also desires peace, we are a further guarantee to you that peace will persist. You are an investment in the future; you represent jobs for our workers. We have no desire to forgo that. It is not espionage that we are offering, it is our mutual futures in lasting peace and cooperation."

Gvashvili smiled.

"It amuses me to listen to you businessmen. And if one day there should be war, we would be better armed thanks to you. But that of course does not bother you."

"Mr. Chairman, we need each other. It's as simple as that."

"Quite so, Mr. Herscu, quite so."

Gvashvili stared straight ahead a moment.

"Well, Mr. Herscu, let me make the following proposal. You will find it, I think, very fair. We will sign the contract once you have installed NATO's UNICOM complete with the apparatus that permits us to intercept freely. On the day we are satisfied that the device works properly, we will jointly sign the formal protocol of agreement. Until then we will continue our negotiations. Should anything go wrong, you lose your contract and we lose our ear in NATO since I imagine you can disconnect your end of it without undue difficulty. So we both stand to gain and we both stand to lose. Equitable?"

The two men shook hands.

"Perfect. Just in time, too, as I believe we've arrived at your hotel."

Pulling aside one of the curtains, Gvashvili watched Herscu stride through the Hotel Moskva entrance.

The chairman had not been entirely truthful with Herscu. He should have added that if anything did go wrong, Herscu would never leave the USSR.

Gvashvili did not trust CONSERV. Not just because, once before, CONSERV had tried to trick the Soviet State. Rather, CONSERV's entire past aroused in Gvashvili a suspicion bordering on loathing.

It had something to do with the fact that Gvashvili, as a Great Russian whose entire family had been slaughtered by the Germans, found it difficult to like traitors. Even more so when they clothed their treachery in economic garb.

". . . Fortress Blue, ending now."

Nicolas Ross heard Herscu's signal fade out and die. Ross rubbed his hands together contentedly.

The Russian contract was as good as signed!

He decided to celebrate the occasion with a small glass of sherry. As he poured out the amber liquid, he was conscious of a great feeling of relief. That goddamned Vardney had almost ruined . . .

Ross raised the crystal glass and sipped.

But he always won in the end. And once again he had outmaneuvered Vardney. Still, it surprised him that Vardney had had the intelligence to try to defect to the French. On the European terrain and in the Middle East, the French electronics firms were fierce competitors to CONSERV-GTT. A clever move Vardney had made.

Nicolas Ross did not like to admit he made mistakes, but it annoyed him to feel he had underestimated Vardney's slyness.

It won't happen again, Ross told himself. As soon as Vardney was returned . . .

The meeting took place in the United States Embassy on l'avenue Gabriel. There were three men in the room.

The CIA station-chief in Paris was piqued that Porter, his counterpart in England, had seen fit to fly over in person. He felt infringed upon. All the more so because the director himself had authorized Porter's unwelcome presence on this side of the Channel.

Fuming inside, Bryant, the CIA chief in Paris, listened to Porter's droning monotone.

". . . and that, gentlemen, is what is expected of us. Stu, I'm only here to pick up delivery so it's your show as to how it's done."

Porter looked at Bryant who had nervously been spinning a pack of Tareytons on the table.

"Well, I've got a good thing with the French here and I'm not going to bugger it up snatching someone from under their noses," Bryant said sourly.

"Stuart," Porter said evenly, "no one's asking you to bugger anything up. They have a man I want. Just get me the man."

The third man in the room now spoke.

"It's an easy matter for us to go outside on this one. Paris has no shortage of contract help."

"A very good suggestion, Mr. Price," Porter said.

Bryant glowered at Price.

"Well, Stuart," said Porter, "will you be satisfied if we go outside? If I understand you, you're only worried about saving face vis-à-vis the French. Unless you object to this in principle?"

Bryant stopped fidgeting with his cigarettes. He'd made his point. There was nothing to be gained by overdoing it.

"Oh, very well. It's fine with me if we go outside. But I want someone we've never used in France before."

Price opened the gray folder over which he had folded his hands.

"I don't want some musclebound brute for this," Porter said. "I want someone who can think for himself but who can use force if it proves necessary. After all, this SDECE agent, Blake, may be amenable to an understanding."

Price flipped through the folder rapidly, then turned back a couple of pages.

"Here's someone interesting. What do you think?" He passed the folder around.

Even Bryant was impressed with the man's qualifications.

"A *ninja*—that's a brilliant choice," Porter said. "And he never uses a gun?"

"Never," Price confirmed.

"I've seen that name before," Bryant said.

"It's Ho Chi Minh's old *nom de guerre*," Price explained.

"So it's decided then?" Porter said.

Stu Bryant nodded.

"You'll get in touch with this fellow and he'll set it all up? I think it best if we don't take too long on this. You can tell the man that we want results quickly.

"There's no need for me to stay in Paris. Stu, call me one day before delivery and I'll fly over to pick up the package. Good day to you both and I'll be hearing from you, Stu, soon."

"Arrogant bastard," Bryant said after Porter had gone.

Price looked at his chief and said nothing.

"You'll be case officer on this, Walt," Bryant went on. "I just don't want any trouble with the French, understand? And if things look like they're beginning to screw up, I want to be first to know about it."

Walter Price nodded.

"What have we got on this Blake? What a name for a Frenchman!"

Price reached down for his attaché case and produced another file.

"Just the bones. His father's a Brit—that's why he has an English name, by the way. Two of our people are keeping an eye on him to get an idea of his habits. As soon as we have a better picture, I'll meet with the 'casual.' "

"How do you pronounce that name?" Bryant asked.

"Nguyen Ai Quoc," Price said slowly.

The afternoon was bright and windy when Walter Price, looking very businesslike in his gray suit and carrying his attaché case, pulled open the door of the An-Vietnam Restaurant on la rue d'Arras.

Inside, the places were already laid out for the evening. The light was dim. The candles on the table had not yet been lit.

Price sat down at the bar and ordered an Armagnac.

He drank slowly.

The sound of dishes and animated conversation came from the kitchen at the rear. Occasionally a waitress would look out to see if there was anyone at the tables.

It was early still.

At the bar, Price was attempting to recapture something in his memory. The noises and odors of Saigon. The frenzy. The passions of that enormous con-game that had been the Republic of Vietnam.

He wasn't succeeding. This was Paris. The other no longer existed.

"Is the boss around?" Price asked suddenly in Vietnamese. For a moment the bartender's face reflected his astonishment, then the almond eyes grew black and fathomless.

"I'll see," he replied quietly and walked toward the back of the restaurant.

He returned followed by another man of indeterminate age who walked with the litheness of a cat.

"Walter!"

The American and the Vietnamese embraced. Price felt Ai Quoc's body as hard as steel. He knew perfectly well that had the other borne him any malice, he would not have come out of the embrace alive. Ai Quoc could have so easily snapped Price's spine.

"You sonovabitch! What are you doing here?" Ai Quoc switched to pure American.

He was somewhere between thirty and forty. His face was both young and old. He had hardly changed. Same thin nose and delicate mouth. High cheekbones and jet-black eyes. The long scar across his throat.

Price smiled and for a moment wished he had not come on business. It would have been nice just to talk.

"I'm working out of Paris now," he said.

"Same trade?" Ai Quoc asked.

"Same trade."

A sadness crossed the Vietnamese's features.

"And that's why . . .?"

"That's why, little brother."

Ai Quoc's face hardened slowly.

"Walter, let's go sit in a corner over there. You want tea?"

"According to our information, you're still active. Are you?"

Ai Quoc raised his teacup.

"Sometimes. A man has to keep fit even when he no longer needs the money."

THE DOUBLE-CROSS CIRCUIT 89

"I have something. Do you want to hear about it? If you don't, say so and we'll forget the matter. It's up to you."

"Go ahead, Walter. I'm curious to know what you do with your talents nowadays."

Price explained the problem. He spoke for about ten minutes. When he had finished, Ai Quoc asked:

"This Blake, do you have a folder?"

Price opened his attaché case.

For what seemed a long time, Ai Quoc stared at the photographs of Blake taken in the Paris streets by the CIA.

"So that's him," Ai Quoc said finally.

"That's the one."

Price stared at Ai Quoc, whose eyes were totally black, their expression very distant.

Price knew that in putting forth Ai Quoc's name he had chosen well. Ai Quoc would convince Blake. And if it proved necessary, Ai Quoc would kill Blake. To Ai Quoc, there was very little difference between talking to a man and taking his life.

What made him so frightening at times was that he killed not out of enjoyment or because it was a job that needed doing. Ai Quoc killed out of philosophic duty. To him, the condition of Death represented the true harmony of the universe.

Nine

BLAKE TORE open the brown envelope and dumped the contents onto his desk. He saw very quickly that the responses were short.

Nothing.
Niente.
Nul.
Nothing.
"Shit!"

Using his thumbnail, Blake slit the Tobacco Board's seal on the pack of Gitanes. He lit a cigarette and smoked nervously. His eyes were fixed on the dead man's photograph. His thoughts, directed to the dead man's soul, were far from charitable.

He was getting nowhere.

Also on the desk were various slips of paper. Telephone messages from the SDECE agents he had sent to check with the private clinics where alcoholics who

THE DOUBLE-CROSS CIRCUIT 91

could afford the cure were treated. The agents had had no luck either.

Blake continued to stare morosely at the dead man's photo. After a while, he shifted his gaze and stared morosely toward the window.

Outside, the trees in front of the boulevard Mortier *caserne* seemed black and skeletal. The branches swayed wildly, blown by a wind Blake could neither hear nor feel. The frantic movement of the branches only grated on his nerves.

He picked up the cables once more and stared at them.

Was it possible that no one had ever heard of UNICOM? The cabled replies seemed to suggest that this was indeed the case.

Blake mashed his cigarette in the ashtray and promptly lit another. As he blew out the match, the violence of his breath flipped over two of the cables. Blake frowned then turned over the other two.

On the back of each cable, a clerk in Communications had punched in the time at which the cables had arrived.

The cables from Cheltenham, Rome, and Bonn had been punched in within a span of two hours. This made sense as they would have received them at approximately the same time. From that point it would not have taken long to verify that there was nothing on UNICOM and to reply accordingly.

But it had taken the CIA almost twelve hours to reply!

Blake turned over the cable from Langley and reread it.

REGRET UNABLE PROVIDE INFORMATION UNICOM STOP OUR RECORDS INDICATE NO INFORMATION AVAILABLE WHATSOEVER STOP IF YOU SUCCEED WOULD APPRECIATE COPY DATA UNCOVERED END STOP

So if they had nothing, why take a half-day before letting him know this?

A thought suddenly struck Blake. It was all the more startling because it had hitherto totally escaped him.

He pulled open the desk drawer where he had put the original folder forwarded by Davoli of the Police Judiciaire. He could feel his heart pounding as he lifted out the sheet of paper on which the dead man had written his final message.

He stared at the collection of shaky lines. Now that he knew what to look for, he could see what he had been unable to see before. Blake felt his chest tighten as the lines at last formed a pattern.

The drawing would not have impressed a geographer at all, but that scarcely mattered: the dead man had drawn a map of the USSR!

As a map, it was very poor. Yet there it was: the outline of the Baltic, the border with Poland, the Caspian to the south, and dots for the major cities, Volgograd, Kiev, Leningrad, and Moscow. And it was across this map of the Soviet Union that the man had written the letters UNICOM.

No wonder nobody knew anything about UNICOM!

His eyes bright, Blake looked up at the photograph.

"You son of a whore," he whispered, "you spoke!"

The dead man's eyes continued to stare toward the ceiling.

Blake grabbed his telephone.

"Cerbère! Yes, it's me. Remember my ghost? I think I've got him. I want a run on all the important Soviet scientists and some less important ones if you've got them. I want to know who's fallen out of grace in the last five years and I want lists of the projects these people were working on. Above all, I want their photographs. Everything you've got. Send it up here to my office. That's right."

THE DOUBLE-CROSS CIRCUIT 93

He did not bother to hang up. As soon as he got his tone, he dialed again.

"It's Blake. I want the colonel. . . . Hello, chief? I think I've got him. Who? My dead man! . . . That's the one. Are you ready? Cerbère's getting out the facts so I'll confirm as soon as he sends up the stuff, but what it looks like is a Soviet, a scientist I'd say. I can't begin to guess how he got here but he's telling us something they've got. . . . That's it, the UNICOM. . . . One other thing I'd better tell you about before the pressure starts. I'm almost certain the Americans know. . . . Well, they delayed for twelve hours before answering a routine inquiry. . . . I find that odd, anyway. As I said, I think you can expect some official jealousy from Washington, so tell them to shove it. This Russian is mine!"

Blake hung up.

The first flush of excitement persisted a while longer. But already another emotion had surfaced, sending forth little prickles of doubt that soured the enjoyment. Then he felt a wave of fear clench his stomach.

Blake did not understand why he should suddenly be afraid—all he knew was that he felt abruptly, inexplicably frightened.

As though looking down from the photograph on the wall, the dead man continued to stare.

Walking quickly, Blake passed through the main gates of the SDECE *caserne* and turned left on le boulevard Mortier. Earlier, he had called Cerbère only to be told that the material on the Soviet scientists would not be ready until after two. So Blake had time for lunch at the brasserie nearby on la rue Vidal de la Blanche.

Three RATP buses rumbled past, following each

other closely like elephants. There was a dank odor of rotting leaves in the air.

Blake felt chilly and turned up the collar of his jacket. The wind brought with it an undertaste of winter.

Ahead, a blonde girl was walking in the same direction. She was teetering precariously on spike heels. A priest, nose plunged in a book, passed Blake on the left. Further along a young man in his twenties was holding open a newspaper and peering about.

As Blake drew nigh, he saw that the young man was Indo-Chinese. A student probably.

"Pardon, monsieur. La rue Le Vau?" the young man inquired timidly.

Blake had already turned to point when he realized his error. He felt the hair on his nape react, but his instinct was faster than his mind.

"Very carefully, monsieur," the young Indo-Chinese said softly.

Blake turned and caught a glimpse of the black automatic partially covered by the newspaper. The young man's eyes were like black beads.

"We're going to cross the street now. Don't try to run."

When they had reached the other side, the young man made a gesture with his chin.

"Keep walking and remember I'm behind."

Blake's mind seemed frozen. The message kept repeating itself: "Viets, Viets, Viets," but nothing else.

They came alongside a gray Citroën CS.

"Get in," the young man ordered.

Blake opened the door. In the back was another Viet. Older, with high cheekbones and a narrow nose. He was wearing a dark-blue suit.

Blake sat down next to him. The young man came around to the driver's side and got in. Blake heard a click and realized that all the doors locked automatically as in a police car. The CS moved out into the traffic.

"Mr. Blake," said Nguyen Ai Quoc, "so good to meet you."

Blake stared at the man beside him. The face was not familiar. Blake felt a horrible queasiness in his bowels.

"I don't know you," he murmured, startled by the tightness of his voice.

"As you wish," Ai Quoc replied. "There is no need for alarm. This tête-à-tête will be perfectly amicable."

Blake looked beyond the window at the daily reality outside. His heart had begun to race.

"Who are you? What do you want?"

Ai Quoc smiled.

"Do not be naive, Mr. Blake. You have a simple choice to make: either we proceed in a gentlemanly manner or we proceed by force. Which shall it be?"

"What are you talking about?" Blake suddenly shouted.

Ai Quoc's black eyes fixed him momentarily.

"Mr. Blake, do not be childish."

"Childish, I? No, my friend, it's you. What does it take to make you understand! My God, the war ended over fourteen years ago. Your people were broken and broken again. What the hell can you possible be after now?"

It was Ai Quoc's turn to look puzzled.

"What are you talking about?"

"The goddamned OAS!" Blake yelled. "And the rest of you Mission C people, you and all the other old *barbouzes*."

To Blake's astonishment, Ai Quoc burst out laughing. He laughed so hard his eyes teared.

"Ah, Mr. Blake, I should be insulted. Really. But I

think I begin to understand your confusion. However, rest assured—this has nothing whatever to do with Algeria."

Blake stared. Slowly the nightmare that had haunted him for over fourteen years dissolved.

In the final months of the Algerian war, the SDECE had collaborated with the Organisation Armée Secrète, the rightwing secret army, in a last-ditch attempt to keep Algeria French. The ramifications of this collaboration would last for years. Many SDECE agents went over to the secret army and continued the struggle in France even after the ex-colony had achieved independence. There would be reprisals and counterreprisals, often against SDECE agents who had not been involved. The reprisals went on long after everyone else had forgotten the war itself.

Among the OAS killers were a number of Vietnamese, chosen from the ranks of the Indo-Chinese war "specials," and originally brought to Algiers as part of a secret unit known as Mission C created to fight against the OAS. As with the SDECE, many later changed sides. Those who survived eventually became soldiers for any number of right-wing "lunatic fringe" causes.

It took Blake a while for the truth to sink in. This was not the return of an old nightmare. This was an entirely new one.

Slowly Blake's features grew pale.

"Oh God," he murmured and slumped back in the seat.

A thin smile of satisfaction appeared on Ai Quoc's lips.

"Now that you've understood, Mr. Blake, perhaps we can come to an agreement. You have a man we want. For my side, the matter is quite straightforward: we would like this man returned to us. The only question is whether you're prepared to let us have him back.

"If you agree. we will reward you richly. I am au-

THE DOUBLE-CROSS CIRCUIT 97

thorized to bid very high. As I said earlier, the choice is yours."

As it came to Blake, the thought was almost violent. If they want him back, they must think he's still alive!

"He doesn't want to go back," Blake said.

"Come, Mr. Blake, his personal preferences are not the issue. But yours are. How much would you like? Feel free to name your price."

The dead man's name! He's got to say the dead man's name!

"I need time to think. Besides, his health is delic—"

"There is no time to think, Mr. Blake. I must have your decision now. One hundred thousand francs?"

"Do you know who he is?"

Ai Quoc's black eyes fixed Blake steadily.

"Name your price, Mr. Blake."

It hadn't worked. Ai Quoc thought Blake was holding out for more money.

Blake plunged. There was nothing else he could do for now.

"One million francs and you can have him back."

"I'm glad you are a reasonable man, Mr. Blake."

Colonel Santerre's thin mustache bristled with indignation.

"You had no authority to make such an arrangement, Blake. This is completely ludicrous. Good heavens, even if you succeeded, how long would it take them to discover your man is an imposter? And then what? And who the hell is fool enough to risk his neck for something like this? You still don't know who your dead man is. Impossible, Blake, impossible."

"Chief, I said I saw a chance and jumped for it. This is an opportun—"

"For what? To ask someone to volunteer for a mission

from which there is no escape? This is not your domain, Blake, and you've gone too far. I never should have given this to you to begin with. You're an intelligence analyst—not an operative."

"Well, sir, at least I've gotten somewhere with it."

Santerre snorted.

"Where, I wonder? This is turning into a kamikaze operation. Sorry, Blake, it's out of the question."

"But, sir, can't we get someone out of prison for this. A condemned man and if he succeeds . . . That's been done before."

"Enough, Blake. This is not your domain, I repeat. If only you could identify this fellow of yours, perhaps . . . no, no, I won't hear of it."

"In that case I need an authorization to carry a weapon," Blake said sullenly.

Santerre looked up impatiently, then reached for a form on which he signed his name. He tore it off the pad and handed it to Blake.

"Fill it in yourself. You'll note I'm not taking you off this yet, but for God's sake use a little more judgment."

Blake stiffly left Santerre's office.

"There you go," said Cerbère, handing Blake three bulging files. "Your Soviets."

"You're a prince, Cerbère. But I'll need two more things."

"What?"

"I need the sheets and files on all the men sentenced to death in our prisons plus I want mugs and fact sheets on all Vietnamese ever used by us, either in Indochina or in Algeria or even later."

Cerbère groaned.

"I'll see what I can do."

Blake had spread the files on the Soviet scientists all over the desk. There were more on the floor around his chair. The ashtray was filled to overflowing. Blake's eyes were red.

He flipped open yet another file and stared at the poor-quality photograph.

"Not him either," he murmured.

He had been at it all afternoon. He had looked at hundreds of photographs. None remotely resembled the dead man.

Blake had been so certain he would at last make a match. But once again the elusive truth was slipping beyond reach.

He flipped through another file.

It was dark outside by the time Blake finally accepted the fact that his dead man was most likely not a Soviet scientist.

The Armory was in the subbasement. Blake thrust the form through the small wicket.

"I need an automatic and some ammunition."

He settled on a 9-mm PA-15. Originally a competition pistol, the PA-15 was adopted by the French government for service use. It is a semi-automatic similar to the American .45 and weighs a little over two pounds. The magazine holds fifteen rounds, fired at a muzzle velocity of approximately 1200 feet per second.

Blake hefted the blued metal.

"Sign here," said the man behind the wicket.

After Blake had signed the form, two boxes of ammunition were slid through.

"You can try it out in the range down the hall on the right."

Blake spent the next hour trying out the -15. He was not as rusty as he had expected.

As he left, the weight of the pistol against his ribs made him feel odd. It brought back memories he would rather not have remembered. But he no longer had a choice.

He was in trouble.

Ten

"SAUNDRA, IT'S me . . . No, at the office. I've got to stay late. I may be all night. . . . Well, I don't know . . . Are you expecting anyone? . . . O.K. Be sure to double-lock the door . . . . Me too. 'Bye."

Blake hung up. For a moment he had hesitated. But there was no need to alarm her yet. He still had a little time to play with. Double or nothing.

He picked up the folders and started downstairs.

Cerbère saw by Blake's face that the night was going to be long.

"Nothing, eh?"

Blake shook his head.

"You don't mind that I asked you to stay?"

Cerbère shrugged.

"No, I get overtime. It'll placate the wife."

"You're still a prince. I meant that."

Cerbère briefly looked pleased.

"What's the order of the day? Night, rather," he said.

"Since our man is not a Soviet, let's get started on the other side. I'll stay down here so as not to waste any time."

"O.K.," Cerbère said, "use the desk. I'll have your Death Row faces in a minute. The Viets'll take longer. Meanwhile, I can start on the Americans. You're still with scientists?"

"That's my bet. Try all categories. Not just nuclear."

Presently Cerbère brought Blake the data on the condemned. With each arrest record and trial history was a small two-by-four-inch photograph, smudgily duplicated by photo-electric process.

Blake began going through the stack, glancing at the photo first, then at each man's height and weight.

Of course, Santerre was right. What Blake had in mind was a kamikaze operation. But, like anything, there was always that miraculous chance, that tiny probability ...

Blake sifted through once, pulling out those who would never do. Ten minutes later, he was left with three men. Finally he held the last man's file at arm's length.

His eyes had become so accustomed to looking at the dead man's photo that he had no trouble superimposing his features upon those of this prisoner awaiting the results of appellate proceedings.

"Maybe, just maybe," Blake murmured.

The prisoner's hair would have to be dyed, he would have to lose some weight, the nose was not right but that could be fixed. It could possibly work if he were heavily sedated.

Only now did Blake look at the man's name and record.

Blake's eyebrows rose.

THE DOUBLE-CROSS CIRCUIT

Jean Varennes had been condemned to death three months ago for the sex killing of a four-year-old boy.

Jean Varennes was as good as guillotined.

"Cerbère," Blake shouted, "I'm going out for a couple of hours."

Even in daylight, Fresnes Prison is a lugubrious place, haunted with memories of the Occupation. For it was here the Nazis executed members of the Resistance. By the time Blake arrived it was after lights-out. He followed the assistant director down the long empty corridor that smelled of carbolic soap.

This part of the prison had not yet been equipped with mechanically operated sliding doors *à l'américaine*. The doors of each cell were solid metal with a small peephole at eye level.

The assistant director was elegantly dressed, but his pinched features did not match the fashionable cut of his suit.

"I must repeat, monsieur, that while we are always willing to assist the course of justice, there are certain formalities that need observing."

Blake assured him once again that he would forward the appropriate official papers in the morning.

"Here it is. 714. You can have only fifteen minutes. All those in our charge are entitled by law to their sleep—without exception."

"I quite understand," Blake said soothingly. "I'll knock for you to let me out."

The assistant director unlocked the door.

Jean Varennes had lost some weight since the police photograph was taken. His cheeks were gaunter and

Blake was immediately struck by the increased resemblance to the dead man. Varennes seemed depressed.

"Hello, old man," said Blake, "I've come to see you with a proposal."

Blake was strangely quiet when he returned to SDECE headquarters. Cerbère saw him walk into the room and sit down at the desk.

"Your Viets are there," Cerbère said.

"O.K.," Blake replied without looking up.

Cerbère watched Blake continue to stare vacantly at the untouched folders before him. After several minutes Blake shook himself and began examining the files on the Vietnamese "specials."

But his black mood only deepened as he leafed through the lives of men irrevocably perverted by the course of war, lives in many ways like his own save that these men were all beyond redemption. What was he thinking? He was just like them! Not a whit better. For he had learned tonight that he had forgotten nothing.

It all came back. And so easily that it was hard to belive he had been clean all this time. Clean! Once you've been sullied, you stay that way.

Blake gave no cry of joy when he found the Vietnamese who had sat next to him in the gray Citroën. He recognized the face though the photograph was over twenty years old. Coldly he read the facts that made up the man's life.

Xuan Tien. Codename: Nguyen Ai Quoc. Born: Annam, August, 1930. Father: minor colonial official. Parents murdered by Japanese soldiers, early 1941. Recruited by the Kempetai, Imperial Japan's gestapo, at twelve years old. Turned over to Japanese secret service and trained in the martial art of *ninjutsu*. Sent to Hanoi as agent for Japanese. November, 1948: arrested by Viet

THE DOUBLE-CROSS CIRCUIT

Minh who slit his throat and abandoned him for dead. Reappears March, 1950, in Annamite underworld. Arrested by French police, July, 1951, on suspicion heroin trafficking. Released. Arrested, September, 1953, for prostitute's murder. Recruited SDECE, October, 1954.

The record went on. Selective assassinations on behalf of the SDECE together with a growing underworld reputation. Ai Quoc poured millions of *piastres* into Ngo Dinh Diem's rising star, all the while continuing to work for the French. As the American involvement began, Ai Quoc worked for the new masters too.

By 1958, he was one of the major figures of the Saigon underworld. And then just before Diem's assassination, he cut all his ties with the lucrative world of vice and transferred his fortune to a Swiss account.

His political involvement continued. He was credited with the organization of highly trained killers known as the Black Berets who served as part of the CIA's Operation Phoenix.

Blake did not finish the file on Nguyen Ai Quoc. He had found what he was looking for. He was beginning to have some idea of what he was up against.

Ai Quoc was still in the employ of the CIA—the file made that abundantly clear. Therefore, Blake was certain now that his dead man was American, that the CIA had knowingly lied about UNICOM, that they had hired this Viet killer to retrieve their property, and that it all had something to do with the Russians. And Blake had stumbled into the midst of it.

Of what he did not yet know. But at last he was getting somewhere and he would continue until he had it all.

"Cerbère!" he called out, "that's enough for tonight. Let's go home and sleep."

As Blake crawled into bed next to Saundra, she turned toward him and mumbled sleepily, "What were you doing all this time?"

Blake did not reply until her breathing was regular and she was again asleep.

"Preparing for an execution."

Blake did not sleep very well that night.

"You've got a what?" Santerre shouted, anger making him rise from behind the desk.

"A volunteer," Blake replied evenly. "For the kamikaze operation."

Santerre's eyes appeared to water; his mouth worked soundlessly; he paced back and forth and finally came to a stop in front of Blake. Since Blake was taller, Santerre was obliged to look up, craning back his neck.

"This better be good, Blake," he said harshly.

Briefly Blake related his interview with Jean Varennes. He spoke of the condemned man's desperation, so acute that Varennes was prepared to risk his life even though his chances of making it through were infinitesimal. But even a tiny chance was better than the odds offered by Madame Guillotine. Blake told Santerre he had made Varennes believe he would be pardoned if he agreed to perform this service for the State. Blake said that he himself knew full well Varennes would be killed as soon as the imposture was discovered.

"But Varennes thinks he has a chance of making it through and because of that he'll be a more effective decoy. What he gives us is time, though not more than two days, in which to discover where they will take him. Hopefully the place he is taken to will tell us our next move."

To Blake's surprise, Santerre was no longer angry.

"You know, Blake, I'd always wondered about you after you turned down our offer to go operational in 1963. Why now? What has changed you?"

"I don't know, Colonel, perhaps I'll find that out as I go along."

"Well, it doesn't matter. Still, I'm not convinced of the reasons why the sacrifice of this Varennes is necessary."

Now Blake related what he had discovered about Nguyen Ai Quoc and his growing conviction that this was an American operation that had somehow gone wrong.

"All of our dead man's actions up to his death have been deliberate. Let's assume he could have killed himself in London, or in Copenhagen, or Brussels. He didn't. He *chose* Paris. I'll go so far as to say he wanted to get in touch with us, but he chose his own way of doing it. At the bottom of this, Colonel, there's something in it for us."

"It's possible," Santerre replied, "though that's hardly an argument I can present to the director."

"You mean you'll go along with it?"

"Perhaps, Blake, perhaps. I still want to hear all of your plan, every detail."

"I have to call Nguyen Ai Quoc at seven tonight to arrange for the delivery."

"Very well, Blake, that leaves you all day. I still wish to hear the details of your plan.

When it wants to, the machinery of the administration of justice can operate with great speed. It took only the morning for Operation Kamikaze to become legal, a mere question of an understanding between the director of the SDECE and the minister of the interior. The operation was covered by that magical legal concept known in jurisprudence as *raison d'état*. The actual particulars would have made any self-respecting lawyer scream, but then such cases rarely find their way before the courts.

It was almost two when the official black Citroën with government plates drove through the gates of Fresnes Prison. This time the prison director in person led the party to Varennes's cell and there was no complaining about irregularities.

Jean Varennes was bewildered at the sight of the four men who squeezed into the small area that smelled of urine.

"It's you," he said flatly when at last he recognized Blake.

"You haven't changed your mind, have you?" Blake asked, not bothering to introduce the others with him.

Varennes seemed surprised.

"No."

"That's good because it's all arranged. You'll get your pardon signed by the president of the Republic himself," Blake lied.

Varennes looked as though he had just been awarded a medal.

Standing to the side, Santerre watched Blake, his gray eyes carefully scrutinizing the younger man.

"Varennes, you don't speak English, do you?" Blake asked.

"No, should I?"

"I thought so." Blake nodded to one of the others who opened the black case he was carrying.

"Sit down, Varennes."

The prisoner was suspiciously eyeing the man who had produced a syringe and was filling it from a small bottle of clear liquid.

"It's for the dye for your hair, Varennes," Blake said. "It'll help it take. You won't feel a thing."

Unhappily, Varennes rolled up the sleeve of his coarse

THE DOUBLE-CROSS CIRCUIT

prison blues. Three seconds after the injection, Varennes was out cold.

"Lay him out on the bed," the man said. "Charlie set up your light, then keep administering the drug. Colonel, I cannot guarantee against infection in these conditions."

Santerre only nodded.

The other man, known as Charlie, had also opened his case and was now setting up a bright light on a stand.

"Blake," the first man said, "forget about his nose, eh? It'll never set in so short a time."

"That's right. Just plant the thing under his skin. Don't cut deeply; there's no point. After, do what you can for his looks."

The "thing" was a small high-power directional finder with a range of 250 miles. It was to be sewn into Varennes's skin. The pulsations emitted from the finder would enable the SDECE to pinpoint the location of the man after he was turned over to Nguyen Ai Quoc.

An hour and a half later, the transformation was complete. The electronic directional finder was activated and inserted in the fleshy bulge around Varennes's waist. Then, working from the photograph of the dead man provided by Blake, the SDECE doctor dyed Varenne's hair a similar sandy color and grayed the temples. With various injections he slightly altered Varennes's facial structure, puffing out the skin over the cheekbones to make the face seem more hollow.

"The effect will diminish after forty-eight hours," the doctor said glumly.

"It'll be sufficient," said Blake.

In a bad light, the resemblance was fair except for the nose: Varennes's was pulpy, the dead man's narrow. About that, nothing could be done. There just was not enough time.

"Be sure he stays unconscious," Blake said, staring at

Varennes now dressed in clothes similar to those in which the dead man had been found.

"Don't worry," the doctor replied. "He'll get another shot just before he's picked up and it'll keep him out for a good long time."

The equipment was put away and the black bags snapped shut. Santerre rapped on the cell door.

"An ambulance will come early tonight to get him," Blake said to the prison director who operated the door. "Until then, no one is allowed to see him. No one at all, understand?"

It was exactly seven o'clock in the evening when Blake reached into his pocket for the slip of paper on which Ai Quoc had written the number to be called.

Blake dialed slowly. Inside the central office for that exchange, a SDECE crew was standing by to try to race the number Blake was calling.

A voice Blake did not recognize answered.

"735-20-21."

"This is eight-zero." He was repeating what Ai Quoc had told him to say.

"Eight-zero, be at the Porte d'Orléans overpass for the service road running into the autoroute for the south in one hour from now. How will you be identified?"

"I'll be driving a red-and-white ambulance. I'll be alone except for the patient. And you?"

The line went dead.

Blake depressed the button several times to get the attention of the crew at the central office.

"Anything? . . . Too short, that's what I thought. Thanks."

Blake turned to Santerre.

"Clever buggers. They're probably already there. They'd know it if we sent anyone over now."

"We'll try to follow you as discreetly as possible. Anything from Cerbère yet?"

"Nothing. He's all alone. I need more men to assist him."

"We'll see who can be spared."

"I'd better be off," said Blake, getting up.

He pulled the PA-15 from the shoulder holster and checked the ammunition clip. He jerked back the slide and heard a click as the slug was fed into the firing chamber.

Eleven

It was raining lightly. Under the Porte d'Orléans overpass, a steady stream of cars raced southward, tires hissing against the asphalt.

On the overpass, Blake sat in the driver's seat of the ambulance. Every so often he leaned forward to wipe away the humidity that condensed upon the windshield. He felt cold and wanted to smoke. Behind him, Varennes lay strapped into the portable stretcher. Still unconscious, he did not make a sound.

Blake glanced at his watch. It was after eight. They were being very cautious.

Somewhere to the rear, a car carrying Santerre and three others sat alongside the curb while the occupants surveyed Blake's position through night binoculars.

Blake shivered and once again wondered what would happen when Ai Quoc appeared. Would he go through with the transaction or not?

Ai Quoc had no reason to trust Blake. No reason at all

save for the comforting cynical principle that all men have a price. And Blake had agreed to return the man in exchange for one million francs.

Because of the frosted rear windows of the ambulance, Blake did not see the gray Citroën pull up behind. A moment later, the door against which he was leaning was suddenly wrenched open and Blake almost fell onto the puddle-blotched pavement.

It was the same young man of the day before and he was holding the same 9-mm Cao Dai.

The young man climbed in next to Blake. Simultaneously Ai Quoc got in on the other side.

"Punctual and alone, Mr. Blake," Ai Quoc said. "Very commendable."

Blake felt an attaché case being placed on his knees.

"Count it, Mr. Blake. We don't want any grumbling about being short-changed.

Blake snapped open the case and slowly began to count the wads of bills. He could feel the Cao Dai's muzzle poking into his kidneys.

Ai Quoc turned and reached through the glass panel. He shone a pocket flashlight onto Varennes's features.

"How long will he be sedated?"

"Until tomorrow morning," Blake replied.

He closed the case.

"The sum is correct."

Ai Quoc opened the ambulance door.

"Please, get out, Mr. Blake."

As Blake stood on the wet sidewalk, Ai Quoc climbed back into the ambulance.

"One last thing, Mr. Blake, if anything goes wrong, one of my men has been watching your woman and if he does not hear from me, he has been ordered to kill her."

The ambulance motor turned over and followed by the gray Citroën driven by a third man, the two cars moved away and disappeared down the autoroute service road.

A cold rain spattered against Blake's face.

The SDECE car's brakes squealed loudly. Blake got in next to Santerre and handed him the attaché case.

"For the pension fund."

The joke did not amuse Santerre.

"Driver," he snapped, "back to headquarters!"

In Communications, the large electronic board took up almost the entire wall. The board was a highly sophisticated version of the directional maps that exist for the Paris métro.

The board showed all of Paris and the *banlieux* areas. But everyone in the room was watching a single red dot moving slowly toward the center of the capital.

The red dot represented the directional finder sewn into Varennes's midriff.

"You were right, Blake," said Santerre, "they seem to be heading toward place de la Concorde."

L'avenue Gabriel runs into place de la Concorde.

Outside the American Embassay on l'avenue Gabriel, Porter and Walter Price saw the ambulance go by without stopping. But the red light on the roof flashed briefly, then was extinguished.

Moments later, the gray Citroën pulled up. Ai Quoc was now seated in the back.

"It's him?" asked Porter as he and Price got in next to the Vietnamese.

Ai Quoc nodded.

The gray Citroën picked up speed, racing to catch up to the ambulance.

THE DOUBLE-CROSS CIRCUIT

"They didn't stop," Santerre repeated almost reproachfully.

"So?" said Blake. "They went right past, didn't they?"

The red dot continued down the Champs-Elysées toward place Charles de Gaulle, formerly place de l'Etoile and renamed to commemorate the man of the eighteenth of June.

The red dot turned into l'avenue Marceau. Blake saw Santerre start and knew why. At the junction of l'avenue Marceau and l'avenue Georges-V stands the embassy of the People's Republic of China.

Both men now wondered whether the missing piece of the puzzle was about to fall into place.

They watched the red dot move down l'avenue Marceau, taking an inexorably long time.

Suddenly the dot turned left into l'avenue du Président Wilson.

"Damn," Santerre murmured, "where are they going?"

Inside the tower at the small Villacoublay aerodrome, the night traffic controller faced an unusual problem and was not certain how to handle it.

"Hello C-454, can you not make it to Le Bourget? Your request is most unusual. We are not cleared to receive military aircraft."

The pilot of C-454 once again repeated his request. His French had a heavily American twang.

"C-454 to tower. Request permission to land. This is C-454 to Villacoublay tower."

The controller was all alone. He had to take the responsibility himself. Yet the law was clear: foreign military aircraft were not allowed to land here. On the other hand, if C-454 crashed, the controller would have to live with the knowledge that it was his fault.

The controller made his choice.

"All right, C-454, you can come in on runway 2-L. Are you in mechanical difficulty? Shall I alert the fire-fighting crews?"

"C-454 to tower. Coming in on runway 2-L. No need to alert fire-fighting crews. It's just a small problem I can fix on the ground."

The controller scratched his head.

He directed the American Air Force transport plane in on visual.

Standing up, he watched the plane taxi along the runway and come past the tower, only to continue moving onto the other runway usually used for takeoff.

Then to his amazement he saw two cars, an ambulance and a gray Citroën, race by and drive out to the waiting plane. He saw the ambulance doors open and a form on a stretcher being carried by three men toward the plane.

The controller's telephone began to ring shrilly.

"Yes?" The controller's eyes grew wide. "What? . . . But . . . No, I understand . . . C-454. American. From the NATO base near Cologne. . . . I'll try."

He adjusted his throat microphone.

"C-454, this is tower. You are ordered to remain on the ground by the . . ."

The response was a blast of prop wash from the transport as it readied to takeoff.

"C-454, you are on unauthorized takeoff! C-454, can you hear me?"

There was no reply from the plane.

The controller picked up the phone.

"It's taking off! Shall I alert the air force?"

The voice calling from Paris said 'no,' nor was the controller to mention this incident in his duty log.

The controller hung up.

"Incredible," he murmured to himself," and I thought such things only happened in the movies!"

THE DOUBLE-CROSS CIRCUIT

In the Communications Room, the board now showed a map of France. The red dot was moving toward Normandy in the direction of the coast.

"England," Santerre said, "they're headed for England." He rubbed his hands together. "Well, Blake, I think the director should find all this most interesting."

Blake was still watching the dot as it left French territory for the blackness of the Channel.

"Colonel," he said, "how about having our London people meet the plane when it lands?"

"Certainly, Blake," Santerre replied, "if you can tell me where in England the plane is going to touch down."

Nicolas Ross's black Rolls-Royce came to a stop before the main building of the private airfield in Ashford, Kent. The night air was cool and as was not the case in London where the sky was a perpetual yellow, the stars were clearly visible.

Ross climbed out and paced back and forth to stretch his legs. The thought that soon he would be seeing Vardney filled him with a dull rage.

Had he pursued his anger with the troublesome scientist to its culminating point, he would have had to admit to himself that Vardney did not deserve to live a day longer.

Unfortunately, Ross still needed Vardney. Even after all these years, he was just as dependent on the scientist as he had always been.

But not for much longer. Vardney had almost reached the limit of his value to Ross. Soon Ross could be rid of him at last. But only after the UNICOM modifications were completed. And then Vardney would disappear for all time and Ross would finally be free.

The faint sounds of the transport's engine reverberated

through the stillness of the night. Searching the sky, Ross saw the airplane's lights in the distance.

The transport had already taken off again, headed for its final destination at one of the American bases in the north of England.

In the brightness of the Rolls-Royce's headlights, Ross saw Porter and another man approach slowly across the runway. The two men were carrying a third, holding him under the armpits. This man's feet dragged.

Ross began walking toward them.

"There you are," Porter called out. "Give us a hand; he's a dead weight."

Ross stood still, staring at the drugged figure.

Ross's face began to twitch.

"Ross!" Porter shouted but did not finish his sentence as he noticed the CONSERV director's expression.

"Ross, what's the matter?" Porter added, suddenly alarmed.

"That isn't him," Ross said, and his voice was almost inaudible.

Twelve

THE LITTLE girl was happy. In the beginning, when her parents first told her they would be leaving London to live in Kent, she was very unhappy.

It was going to be horrid, she thought, to move away from her friends and the red buses and the great city where she was born. But, to her surprise, she had discovered it was not horrid. It was true that she had to make new friends out here and her friends here were a very different sort from what her city friends had been.

The little girl paused and listened.

All around her, the stillness of morning crackled. The ground, still wet with dew, was covered with mist in the hollow spots. A faint light like gossamer threads appeared through the trees, weaving the forest together into a gigantic web that floated above her head.

Here, among the fallen leaves of autumn, under the damp branches that had broken off the trees, were her friends, the animals of the woods. And every morning, before leaving for school, she came for a walk by herself to seek out the creatures.

The little girl resumed her walk, moving as silently as possible. Suddenly a twig snapped beneath her foot. In the tree above, there was a quick fluttering of wings and she saw the most beautiful red bird dart into the light.

The little girl began to run, hoping to see the bird again. After a while she forgot about the bird completely.

She continued to run, her arms stretched outward. In the morning coolness, she had become the bird. She was free as only a child knows how to be.

Eventually she stopped and stood still, panting. A small cloud of condensation rose from her mouth into the air.

She was standing at the top of a low gully filled with brown and dark-red leaves from the surrounding trees. Her bright eyes scanned the cushion of leaves and for a moment she wondered whether she should leap down and bury herself among them.

Then she saw the arm protruding.

She uttered a cry, turned, and ran, but after several steps she halted and looked back. She hesitated, her face reflecting puzzlement. Slowly she walked back to the edge of the gully and began the descent.

The arm struck out of the leaves like a drowned man's. The fingers, with dirt under the nails, were twisted in a claw.

Biting her lip, the little girl knelt beside the arm and like a small dog she began to scratch away the leaves.

Except for her father, she had never seen a naked man before. She thought it strange that anyone would go out without any clothes on on such a cold morning, nor could she understand why anyone would keep his head under the leaves. It occurred to her that maybe a person could drown in leaves just as in water.

THE DOUBLE-CROSS CIRCUIT 121

The man was lying face downward with his arm held up.

"Mister," she said, "wake up!"

The man did not reply. The little girl was beginning to feel frightened by the silence around her.

"Mister, please wake up!"

She grabbed onto his arm and pulled. He was so heavy. It took an incredible effort on her part to turn him over.

Simultaneously she saw the open staring eyes and the gaping slash across his midriff. Most horrifying of all was the dangling blue-gray intestines that hung from the hole in his stomach and quivered like a tangle of snakes.

The little girl screamed.

Cerbère watched the sheets of printout spew from his machines. They were Blake's American scientists.

Cerbère did not envy the job of cross-correlating that now faced the brown-haired intelligence analyst.

Cerbère had known Blake for several years, not well but in that way that people who work together get to know each other. Cerbère liked Blake. He had had occasion to meet a great many of the SDECE's people and Blake had always struck him as different. Unlike so many others, Blake did not take himself seriously and Cerbère admired that. It was difficult in this line of work not to take oneself seriously.

Cerbère himself, though he sometimes wondered what was done with the information his machines provided, had developed an attitude of remote indifference to his work. Perhaps it was a way of protecting himself. He wasn't sure.

But Blake's attitude was different. Blake seemed to laugh about it all inside. It showed in his eyes. Those brown mocking eyes that constantly appeared to deflate the overblown egos so common among many SDECE people.

Yet over this miserable suicide who did not have an identity anywhere, Cerbère had seen Blake change. Blake's eyes had ceased to laugh.

Blake was succumbing like the others had to the belief in his own omnipotence, and the more the identity of the dead man eluded him the stronger grew Blake's faith that he and he alone could eventually track the fellow down.

It was too bad, Cerbère told himself. Why couldn't Blake have left well enough alone?

Cerbère sighed softly as he lifted out a stack of printouts from one of the machines. He carried the pile to the desk and placed them in the center before the metal chair. He looked at his watch. Blake had called earlier to say he would be down to go through the material as soon as it was ready. Cerbère gazed at the pile on the desk and shook his head.

"For what?" he asked himself aloud.

And yet the answer was only a meter away. In the very pile he had just placed on the desk.

Thirteen

BLAKE ANGRILY slammed the door of the apartment. He was tired and exasperated with himself and he was beginning to feel jittery.

He had grossly miscalculated. Not for a second had he assumed that Varennes would be taken out of France. He had been certain the trail would lead him somewhere in France.

Instead, twenty-four hours earlier, he had watched the red dot that was Varennes leave French territory in the direction of England. Out of reach and out of sight.

The red dot had disappeared somewhere in the southwest of England, where, because the SDECE board did not have a proper map of the UK, it was impossible to pinpoint with accuracy. And then the signal was lost completely.

A total failure and the needless sacrifice of one man. That was what Blake had earned for himself.

Santerre had not shared his anger. But then Santerre

had an altogether different point of view involving the latitude which Western secret services permit each other within their respective territories. The shadow diplomacy of the shadow world, none of which was Blake's concern.

Still trying to identify his dead man, Blake had hoped to use Varennes as a decoy to trace back the dead man's identity. He had hoped that the location to which Varennes was taken would provide him with a tangible lead.

Instead he had lost Varennes.

He had spent all day working through the printouts on American scientists provided by Cerbère. He had gone through half the stack and still there was nothing.

How much longer did he have? Had Varennes's imposture been discovered?

Blake knew the reprisal would be imminent and that he was the target now.

Saundra was in the shower.

He stood in the bathroom staring at her figure through the shower curtain.

"Is that you?" she called out.

"Yes."

"My, we sound grumpy tonight! Can you hand me the towel, I'm nearly through."

She stood before him, her breasts pink and glistening, her long hair hanging wetly down her back.

"Will you get out of here?" she said, smiling at him. "The steam'll only make your clothes more rumpled."

He went and sat at the kitchen table, staring at the lights of Paris that showed through the windows. He reached inside his jacket and took out the -15, which he placed on the table.

THE DOUBLE-CROSS CIRCUIT 125

Several minutes later, Saundra joined him, wearing a silk kimono. She had wrapped her hair in a towel.

She saw the gun and peered at him curiously.

"What's that here for?" she asked. He could tell by her voice that she was angry at him for having brought the gun into the house. She had never wanted to see a weapon again.

"The usual reasons," he replied. "Saundra, listen to me. Something is happening or is going to happen. I don't want you around when it does. So when your hair is dry, pack some clothes and I'll take you to the train station. I want you to go stay with your parents in Marseilles for a while."

She looked at him a long time. He saw that her knuckles were white.

"What is it?" she asked finally.

"Do you really want to know?"

He saw the tear run down her cheek.

"You promised me," she said, her voice breaking.

"This was not my intention," he replied quietly. "I . . . it got out of control."

She was crying now. Silently.

"You're still with the *Tordus*, aren't you?"

Blake felt ashamed. He nodded.

"You're a first-rate bastard, you know that?"

His eyes glistened but he smiled.

"I was born one."

She wiped her cheek.

"That's not what I meant and you know it."

She turned away and he saw her shoulders tremble. He wanted to get up and hold her. He continued to sit at the table; his arms and legs felt leaden.

"I'm not going," she said finally.

"Saundra . . ."

"You listen to me! You're not going to spirit me out

of here as though I were your gun moll. You want to be tough, then you can protect me with your popgun for tonight. I'll go in the morning and I'm not coming back. I think you've made your choice, and it doesn't include me."

She walked from the kitchen. He heard the bedroom door close.

He continued to sit at the kitchen table. He stared at the -15 lying on the checkered tablecloth as his own tears filled his eyes and overflowed.

In the silence of the night, the first of the two double-locks on the door of Blake's apartment turned slowly. There was not a sound.

Outside the door, Nguyen Ai Quoc worked carefully in the darkness of the hallway. Using an instrument that resembled a perfume atomizer with a long needle-thin nozzle, he had carefully sprayed a jet of oil inside the two locks. He was able to pick the first lock with no difficulty.

Wearing the *shinobi shozoku* of the *ninja*—a black pajamalike outfit consisting of a jacket, a hood, specially designed trousers, and lightweight floss-bottomed shoes—he was unrecognizable.

Ninja means "stealer in," and *ninjutsu* is the ancient Japanese art of the military spy into whose secrets he had been initiated while still a youth by the conquerors of his homeland. From feudal times until the modern era, the exploits of the *ninja* as spies, saboteurs, and psychological terrorists were legendary. The *ninja* evoked such fear in their adversaries that whenever one of the "stealers in" was captured he was horribly tortured and maimed. However, the capture of a live *ninja* was a rare event; they usually managed to kill themselves first.

THE DOUBLE-CROSS CIRCUIT 127

Ai Quoc began on the second lock. His face was hidden by the black hood he wore to muffle his breathing. As an additional precaution he had taped special paper over his mouth.

Around his waist, he carried a leather kit that contained all the equipment he would need. Attached to his belt was a rope of great tensile strength with which he could climb down the side of a building.

Though unarmed in the usual sense of the word, he was not defenseless. His entire being was keyed to and concentrated upon Death.

The second lock turned open as easily as had the first. Again he inserted the nozzle and doused the two hinges of the door. Only then did he ease the door open slightly. His hand moved slowly along the frame searching for a chain lock. There was none.

The door opened just enough for Ai Quoc to squeeze his body through. Once inside the apartment, he lowered himself to his knees, gently closing the door with his foot.

On all fours like a stalking cat, Ai Quoc advanced slowly into the apartment. His eyes searched the darkness, noting the position of the furniture.

He paused and listened, taking in every sound. He could hear the noise of the refrigerator motor, a clock, and the muffled rumbling that Paris makes at night.

He waited until he heard the faint rustling sound of two sleeping humans. Had either of them been awake, even pretending to sleep, Ai Quoc could have detected the difference. In sleep, a person's joints creak ever so lightly. A person awake makes no sound save that of his breath.

Now Ai Quoc knew that both Blake and Saundra were sound asleep. He also knew there was no one else in the apartment, either human or animal.

Still on all fours, Ai Quoc moved toward the bedroom.

Blake was sleeping with his clothes on. The PA-15 rested on his stomach, the butt of the automatic loosely held by his hand. Beside him, Saundra lay under the sheets, still wearing her kimono.

Had Blake suddenly awakened, he could not have seen Ai Quoc from the bed. Lying flat against the floor, Ai Quoc crawled toward the bed.

He was neither tired nor nervous. He had stood in rooms in Vietnam, a meter from his victim, while the latter telephoned, read, and finally settled down for his last night on this earth. Once, a man had suddenly risen to go to the bathroom. Almost invisible, Ai Quoc had waited for the man to ease his bladder, then return to his bed only to die an hour later.

Ai Quoc had to look up once to see who was where. The sight of Blake and the automatic made him smile. Only the dishonorable relied on firearms.

Ai Quoc inched around to the side. He was now between the window and the bed. Lying on his stomach, he pressed up on his arms until his face was only several inches from Saundra's.

He looked at her carefully, suddenly saddened by the fact of her beauty. He felt a deeply poetic grief pass through him like an icy caress and his jet-black eyes appeared to become even darker.

In his mind, he recited a Buddhist prayer for the soul of the dead; then he quickly reached out and touched her.

Even in sleep she recognized that the hand was foreign to her. She scowled and made a noise in her throat and, as he had expected her to, shifted positions, turning onto her back.

THE DOUBLE-CROSS CIRCUIT 129

Ai Quoc opened the leather satchel by his waist and took out two objects. The first was a star-shaped throwing blade known as a *shuriken;* each of the points was tipped with a deadly poison made from cobra venom. The second object he placed on the floor.

Not touching Saundra's skin this time, he opened the kimono, exposing the dark triangle of her pubic hair and the rounded stomach.

Tightly holding the *shuriken*, he pressed one of the points into her stomach and slashed upward.

She twitched once like someone having a bad dream. Within three seconds Saundra was dead.

Ai Quoc dropped the second object into the opening in her abdomen.

Without shifting his position he moved backward lizardlike, returning as he had entered. He closed the apartment door as he left and bounded silently down the winding stairs.

In all, it had taken him not quite an hour.

Blake opened his eyes. The light of morning reflected grayly on the ceiling.

He felt stiff and dirty as one always does after sleeping in one's clothes. He stretched and groaned, then sniffed the air. It was curiously heavy. Cloying. Almost sweet.

Rubbing his eyes, Blake sat up. As he was stretching a second time he saw the blood. It had soaked her pale kimono crimson. It had soaked into the sheets. It was all over her thighs.

And from the hole slashed in her abdomen protruded the wires of the directional finder Blake had had placed in the condemned Varennes.

"Saunndddraaaa!"

It was a howl, screamed from the depth of his soul. It echoed and reechoed and reverberated, tearing him apart. In the ragged sounds that tore from his throat were compressed all his memories of their past together—fatally, violently, irrevocably past.

Eventually he stopped screaming. Out of breath, in pain, his eyes wild, he stared at her as the silent tears streamed down his cheeks. Then he fell heavily to his knees, his head bowed, a man at his own beheading, waiting for the caress of the axe.

And there was none. Only the alien sounds of his whimpering that he listened to in anguish as one might to those of a wounded animal.

He must have knelt for a long time. Oblivious to the ache in his knees, absorbed in the dissection being performed within his heart, he sat completely still. His tears dried, tightening the skin of his face. His lips, split where he had bitten into them, hardened. The light in his eyes slowly diminished as they seemed to glaze over, and the pupils congealed as though frozen like the eyes of the dead man on his office wall.

Finally Blake got to his feet. He approached the bed and his hand shook as he pulled the directional finder out of her and thrust it into his pocket. He then covered her with the sheet, after a final look at her features so tranquil and already so cold.

Blake lurched into the kitchen and rummaged around under the sink. The can of gasoline was still there from the days when he had had a motorcycle.

He unscrewed the cap and swinging the can about went from room to room, spattering gasoline indiscriminately. When it was still one-quarter full, he placed the can on the floor near the front entrance.

He grabbed his jacket from the floor by the bed and slipped the -15 into his shoulder holster.

Before leaving the apartment, he stood a minute longer by the bed.

Just before closing the front door, he turned on all the

gas jets of the stove. He waited in the hall outside the apartment; then using the door as a shield he fired at the gasoline can.

He was halfway down the stairs when the second explosion hammered through the building. A funeral pyre for Saundra.

Fourteen

Cerbère heard the phone ring. Still watching his machines, he walked to the nearest wall and picked up one of the extensions.

It was Santerre and he sounded angry.

"Have I seen Blake? No sir . . . I mean yes. He was in here earlier but only for a moment. . . . He wanted a file. . . . One of the Vietnamese specials. Xuan Tien. We know him as Nguyen Ai Quoc. . . . Yes, that's right. The restaurant on la rue d'Arras."

It was the lunchtime rush and the restaurant was crowded. Protected by the half-dozen or so people who stood in the vestibule waiting to be seated, Blake was already well inside before Ai Quoc saw him.

Blake violently pushed one of the two men standing in front of him. Ai Quoc was toward the back where he had accompanied a couple to their table.

A young waitress carrying a tray had just emerged from the kitchen.

The PA-15 seemed to materialize in Blake's hand. He fired three times in rapid succession.

There were terrified screams. Tables tipped over as the panic-stricken clientele dove for cover.

The waitress, seeing Blake's gun pointed in her direction, began to shriek hysterically. The tray she held fell, splattering food all over her and onto the floor.

Blake saw Ai Quoc spin and knew he had been hit. Blake lurched into a run, weaving between the tables. Ai Quoc regained his balance, turned, and began moving also. The zinc-plated kitchen doors swung as he disappeared behind them.

"The police! Call the police!" someone shouted.

Blake saw that his third shot had hit the door. He kicked it open, simultaneously shifting to the side. He had time to glimpse three startled cooks, mouths agape.

Blake charged through the doors. One of the cooks had grabbed a kitchen knife.

"Don't!" Blake shouted, raising the -15. The knife clattered to the floor. "Where did he go?"

The three refused to answer. Blake looked for a door. There didn't seem to be one.

Raising his eyes, he noticed a small window high on the wall near the ceiling. It was large enough for a man to squeeze through.

Blake jumped up on a table and leaped. The window swung open unlocked. He pulled himself through, cutting his hands on the rough stone of the exterior wall.

As he stood up he saw a small pool of blood on the ground. This was the way Ai Quoc had gone.

Blake found himself in a narrow alley that stank of garbage and urine. He realized now that the restaurant kitchen was below ground level.

Blake swept the alley. On either side were the backs of

buildings. There were no fire escapes, only drainpipes. He looked up, searching for a bloody mark by the drains. He saw nothing.

He ran, watching the ground. After about thirty meters, he saw a pool of cloudy blood widening in a puddle.

Blake ran faster. He could hear his own blood pounding in his temples. His lungs burned. But the thought of Saundra lying dead made him run harder.

The alley turned to the left and widened. Ahead, there was a high stone wall behind which rose the spires of a church. Ai Quoc was halfway up the wall, clinging to it like an insect, hands and arms spread-eagled.

Panting heavily, Blake fell to one knee. With both hands holding the -15 steady, he fired, aiming for Ai Quoc's leg. He heard a cry, then saw Ai Quoc tumble down.

Ai Quoc was trying to crawl away. His shoulder and left leg were stained with blood. Blake's foot caught Ai Quoc in the stomach. There was a gasp of expelled air and Ai Quoc fell onto his stomach. With his heel, Blake stomped Ai Quoc's left leg. Ai Quoc screamed. He was doubled over, writhing with pain.

Blake turned and looked back. By the bottom of one of the buildings he saw a door. Beside it was a dirt-encrusted window.

He grabbed Ai Quoc by the hair and dragged him back. Ai Quoc moaned and tried to free himself. Blake brought the -15's butt down on Ai Quoc's wounded shoulder. Ai Quoc fainted.

The window appeared to give onto a corridor such as can be found in the basement of apartment houses. Blake tried the door. Locked.

Using his shoulder, Blake forced the door. It opened onto a small room; perhaps a coal cellar once. Now the concierge used it to store the garbage bins.

THE DOUBLE-CROSS CIRCUIT

Blake dragged Ai Quoc inside and closed the door. Under the broken lock was a bolt. He shoved the bolt home.

The room led into a corridor where the tenants of the building had their storage lockers. There was a lot of dust about.

Ai Quoc was still unconscious. Blake slapped him several times. Ai Quoc groaned, then his black eyes opened. The pain made his pupils contract, yet he managed to speak.

"Only cowards use guns."

"And heroes kill women in their beds. Just tell me what I want to hear, you fucking gook. Who hired you and why?"

A gurgling sound issued from Ai Quoc's throat. His eyes closed tight. A sliver of bone from his shattered leg poked through a rip in his trousers.

Ai Quoc had nothing to lose any more.

"The CIA," he gasped, "they wanted to get their man back."

"Names, names, goddamn you!"

"Walter Price of . . . of the embassy here and another man named Porter who's a superior to Price. Porter was not from the embassy."

"An illegal?"

"I . . . I don't think so but he was flying in from outside France."

"And the man they wanted—what was his name?"

"I don't know."

"Who were they working for? Why did they want this man back?"

". . . I don't know."

"You're not helping me," Blake said and hit Ai Quoc's shattered leg with the gun barrel.

Ai Quoc's eyes appeared to bulge out of his head, but he did not scream. His face was sweating profusely.

"What was this man's name? Why did they want him back?" Blake repeated.

"I . . . don't know," Ai Quoc replied, breathing heavily.

"Who ordered you to kill . . ." He could not say her name.

"They were very angry you delivered the wrong man. Price said it was up to me to do as I saw fit."

"And Price gave you this?" Blake took the directional finder from his pocket.

"Yes."

"And killing . . . , that was supposed to make me reasonable?"

"It was to pay you back in kind."

"Have you worked for them before?"

"For Price. In Vietnam."

"Not here?"

Ai Quoc wiped the sweat from his eyes. He shook his head.

"They will easily replace me, Blake. You haven't solved anything this way."

Blake said nothing. He moved near the window and looked out. In the alley he saw two *gendarmes* with drawn revolvers. They were not facing this way.

Blake slid into a crouch.

He turned toward Ai Quoc who was swaying slightly. The Vietnamese had lost a lot of blood.

"What else?"

Ai Quoc opened his eyes.

"I've told you what I know."

"All of it?"

"All . . ."

Blake watched Ai Quoc in silence.

After a while he stood and returned to the window. The *gendarmes* had gone.

Blake lifted the lid off one of the garbage bins and

peered inside. He reached down and took out a bottle, and empty liter bottle of the cheap wine one buys for eighty centimes.

Ai Quoc stared at Blake.

Blake smashed the bottle against the wall and moved closer, clutching the jagged bottle by the neck.

Ai Quoc continued to watch him, an odd smile upon his lips.

"You were trained by the Japanese, Xuan Tien. Now die like one."

Ai Quoc saw Blake's arm arc back. For a moment their eyes held, Blake's suffused with tension, while in Ai Quoc's flickered the infinite sadness of fleeting life. Then the sharp glass began its fatal descent.

Ai Quoc felt no pain. At first. The shard of glass criss-crossed his face, blinding him. He did not see Blake slash his throat, but he felt the warmth of his blood as it bubbled from the severed arteries of his neck.

Blake did not leave until Ai Quoc's twitching had ceased.

Santerre grabbed for his telephone.

"Blake! Where in hell are you? My god, man, what has happened?"

Santerre covered the receiver, then depressed his intercom button. "Hurry and trace this call!"

Blake was in a phone-booth on le boulevard Raspail.

"Listen, colonel . . ."

"You listen to me! Have you gone totally mad? I can only help you if you tell me what happened. Was your apartment plasticked?"

"No, I did that."

"You what?!" Santerre shouted. "The police found the body of your . . . wife in the . . . Did you . . . ?

"No, but I've since evened that score."

"Blake, you've gone too far. The police . . ."

"The police can stuff it! I haven't finished, Santerre. There's a CIA op at the embassy here. Named Walter Price. You'd be wise to pick him up if you can."

"I can't, Blake. You've turned this into a bloodbath. It's become a vendetta for you and that's where we draw the line. Come in, Blake, it's finished."

Santerre's secretary handed him a note. He covered the receiver. "Get a car there right away."

"Santerre, you've got to do this for me. Give me a week to finish this. You can do what you like with me after that. But I must have a week and complete freedom. There will be no more killing. You've got to cover for me, Santerre. Dammit, you know how it is!"

During the Occupation, Santerre's first wife had died under torture at the hands of the Gestapo. Santerre recalled that, choking on his grief over her loss, he had run from the hunters to rejoin the shattered remains of his Resistance network. Yes, he knew how it was.

"Blake, I should never have put you on this . . ."

"One week!"

"I'll see . . ."

Blake slammed down the taxiphone receiver and ran.

By the time the SDECE car reached the booth, Blake was nowhere in sight.

Cerbère looked up and started.

Blake was standing by the door of the computer room. Haggard, with lines beneath his eyes, and wearing a suit which Cerbère had never seen before. Blake was not a man who usually wore suits.

"But," Cerbère stammered, "they're all looking for you."

"Outside; not in here. Don't worry about it."

Blake closed the door.

THE DOUBLE-CROSS CIRCUIT 139

As he came forward, Cerbère noticed that Blake's eyes had completely changed. They had become reptilian. For the first time, Cerbère felt frightened by Blake.

Blake seemed to read his mind.

"No, old man, but don't try to cross me. Where's my stuff?"

"On . . . on the table where you left it." Cerbère pointed to the pile of material on the American scientists.

As though nothing had happened, Blake sat at the table and resumed his examination of the files printed out by Cerbère's machines.

For Cerbère the next few hours were nerve-wracking and interminable.

Blake spoke to him once—to tell him to call his wife and say he was working late. Very late.

More time dragged by.

"Cerbère, why do they remove the photos on some of these?"

"For security reasons."

"Here are eight names with no photos. Get me a cross-reference. There must be a photo somewhere else. Try scientific publications going back to before the war. These are the names: Gottshalk, Peter; Salten, James; Perlmutter, Avram; Tonobe, Hideki; Rohenlohl, Gert; Vardney, Eric; Steinmetz, Karl; and Prosbyschyl, Anton. Got them?"

Glad for something to do, Cerbère wrote down the names, then began feeding the retrieval program into the two big CYBER computers.

It took a good forty minutes. As the electronic memory banks ran through hundreds of thousands of publications dating back to the early 1930s, Blake chain-smoked and paced up and down.

He made Cerbère think of a tiger in a cage.

Finally the printouts appeared.

Except for Tonobe, Rohenlohl, and Prosbyschyl, there

were photos of the others in various publications among the mountains stored by the computers. Cerbère handed the five sheets to Blake. They were still warm from the photoelectric light.

Blake looked at the five faces one after the other. He held one up.

Cerbère saw a fair-haired young man with a long face and a pince-nez.

"From *Scientific American*, August, 1936, an article entitled 'Electromechanical Principles Applied to the Encipherment Process' by Eric Halburton Vardney, Engineering Division, Global Telephone & Telegraph Corporation."

"Is that the man you've been looking for?" Cerbère asked as for a moment he saw a spark illuminate Blake's eyes.

"So you see, he's not a ghost after all. And now, Cerbère, you got a name and a company. I want everything there is on both."

Blake's voice changed its pitch. Cerbère watched him walk rapidly away.

Cerbère felt strangely choked as he realized that Blake was doing something tigers do not. Blake was crying.

In his office at Centre Place Nicolas Ross was on the telephone. He was speaking to Porter at the U.S. Embassy overlooking Grosvenor Square.

"What I want to know, Porter," Ross said testily, "is what you are going to do about it."

"Nothing, I'm afraid."

Porter's ears were still ringing from the tirade he had had to put up with earlier from Stu Bryant, his Paris counterpart. Bryant was livid and for once he had every right to be. In this sense the substitution of Varennes for Vardney had succeeded: the unholy alliance that united

CONSERV and the CIA was now on very shaky ground. The two station-chiefs were feuding openly. Bryant had complained to the director himself, charging that Porter had gone far beyond the limits of his brief and in the process badly soured relations with the French. And Bryant was right—if only because the wrong man had been delivered.

Through Riverside, the CIA director had communicated his displeasure to Porter and ordered the station-chief in Britain to sever his involvement with CONSERV.

"Nothing?" Ross shouted, incredulous.

"That's what I said. You know as well as I that you are only entitled to call upon us in extraordinary circumstances. Well, you did; and we did what we could to help. It's not our fault it didn't work out. Now we're involved more than we should be and that's why we can't assist you further. As of this point you're on your own, Ross. I'm very sorry but that's the way it is. Those are the orders I've been given. Good day, Ross."

Nicolas Ross blurted out a protest but only found himself speaking into a dead line. He slammed down the receiver.

Pacing back and forth, he began to assess the situation.

Once again, everything hung in the balance. No Vardney—no UNICOM modifications—therefore no Russian contract. That was the equation he had to go on.

Ross ceased pacing.

The equation was variable. If he could somehow stall NATO on the one hand and the Russians on the other until he found a means of having Vardney returned. But how?

Ross stared out across the expanse of London.

According to the NATO contract, CONSERV-GTT had to have installed the main UNICOM component at NATO headquarters before the end of the year. What if, for reasons seemingly beyond the company's control, this proved impossible? If one of the GTT factories that supplied the NATO UNICOM equipment suddenly went on strike, would that . . . ? Perhaps it might.

Ross made a note on a yellow legal pad.

The Russian part of the equation was not as simple. How to create a delay and still obtain the contract?

Ross resumed pacing.

Could he not get around Vardney's involvement completely by taking the scientist's plans for the UNICOM modifications directly to the Russians?

It would be complicated but Ross did not see why, given the proper data, Soviet scientists could not design the modifications themselves and CONSERV would install them in the NATO UNICOM.

Complicated and delicate, yes, but feasible.

He would have to go to Moscow and work it out with Gvashvili in person.

Colonel Santerre felt uncomfortable.

Across the room, the director of the SDECE sat behind his large gilded desk and peered lengthily at his uneasy subordinate.

"What I fail to understand, colonel," he said at last, "is how one of your departments whose function is strictly analytical appears mysteriously to have gone operational?"

"*Mon général . . . ,*" Santerre began, but the director of the SDECE held up his hand.

"Yes, I am quite aware that I myself approved your substitution of this convict. Yet I recall you justified this on the grounds it would lead to new information. Instead, we have two murders caused by one of our men, an apartment apparently blown up by the same man, the new prefect of police complaining about noncooperation from us in the matter of one of these deaths, the Air Ministry complaining about illegal goings-on at one of our airports . . . My dear colonel, not only I but the Minister of the Interior as well would very much like to know what the hell you are up to?"

Inwardly cursing Blake, Santerre pointed out that the "goings-on" could better be attributed to the Americans than to any SDECE agents.

"Colonel," the director replied, "if I did not have the utmost faith in your abilities and were your record not as good as it is, I admit I would be concerned. However, I am confident you can provide me with a full explanation of all this that will convince both the Minister and the other members of the Cabinet of the necessity of these curious events. There is a Cabinet meeting at the end of the week; your report would prove invaluable should there be questions raised at that time."

Flushing, Santerre nodded.

"I understand, *mon général*."

He saluted and turned sharply on his heels.

"And, colonel," the director added as Santerre was about to open the door, "it has no doubt occurred to you that the mental stability of this man Blake may be in question, has it not?"

Again Santerre nodded. He had understood.

Fifteen

It was late the same night. Since coming in off the street, Blake had worked steadily.

Once more, the faithful Cerbère brought him a pile of material retrieved from the vast storehouse banks of the machines.

"Find a comfortable corner and go to sleep," Blake said, rubbing his eyes. "This may take a while still."

Cerbère wearily nodded his head as Blake lit yet another of his Gitanes.

Blake rifled quickly through the fresh batch of printouts. Surprisingly, there was a lot on Global Telephone & Telegraph. The SDECE seemed very well informed on the activities of this company. Picking a heading at random, Blake read the words, "GTT, the Algerian Revolution and Sahara Subsoil Mineral Rights." He flipped back several pages. "GTT and Soviet Intelligence: the 1951 Trials." Further back: "Wartime Relations between GTT and the Hitlerian Reich."

"*Banco!*" Blake murmured exultantly.

On Eric Vardney, there were only two pages. The bare bones. And the file abruptly ended in 1948. Strange. Blake began to read.

Eric Halburton Vardney was born September 21, 1911, just outside Savannah, Georgia. His parents were descended from Swedish immigrants who had followed the victorious Union Army in its conquest of the Confederacy.

Vardney's father became public works manager of the minicipality where Eric was born. His mother taught Sunday school. The Vardneys were straight-laced, religious, hard-working. They had their place in the little town. Not at the top of the social heap but close enough to nod stiffly to those who were. The Vardneys were proud of what they were.

There was no doubt that Eric was brought up in a stern but affectionate house. Yet parental affection was not doled out at random; it had to be earned. And the best way for a child to do that was to excel in school.

Which Eric did, graduating high school with the best grades ever awarded in the institution's brief history. Not only did he succeed in making his parents beam with pride, he also managed to win himself a scholarship to Princeton.

His scholastic record and especial brilliance in mathematics guaranteed that the scholarship would be renewed. In the early summer of 1934, Eric graduated summa cum laude with his degree in electrical engineering.

It would have been easy for him to remain in university taking additional degrees. But he chose not to. The Depression had dealt a blow to his father who, too old to begin another career, had found himself replaced by a younger man. The family had already eaten well into their modest savings. Concerned for the future of his parents, Eric decided to seek employment.

He was quickly snatched up by the New York office of GTT. Under the astute reign of its founder, Colonel Nepomucene Wehr, Global Telephone & Telegraph was growing dramatically. Having chewed its way through the Caribbean and South America, GTT was now hungry for markets in Europe. The company was in full expansion and eager to recruit capable young men who showed promise.

Vardney arrived at the best possible moment. Hired by the director of the Telegraph Section, Vardney was promptly put to work on a secret project sponsored by the U.S. Navy.

The project aimed to determine the security of the telegraph, in those days still a revolutionary new invention. The group working on the project soon found that it was a simple matter to read telegraph messages using an oscillograph to measure current fluctuations.

The problem then was how to make the telegraph secure. In trying to come up with an answer, Vardney found the field that would preoccupy him for the rest of his life.

To begin with, he solved the problem using the punched paper tape which runs teletypewriters to whose key characters he electromechanically added pulses. The result, named after him, was the Vardney device, the machine that created "on-line encipherment" whereby encipherment and decipherment were done directly on an open telegraph circuit.

Vardney's invention would prove of great interest to the U.S. Signal Corps. In effect, Vardney had fathered the one-time system of encipherment which, during the war, became the communications life-line for clandestine radio operators working in Occupied territories. The

THE DOUBLE-CROSS CIRCUIT

one-time system was called that because any repetition in the decoding key allows an enemy to decipher a signal. The one-time system used a random, nonrepetitious key only once which, being unpredictable, made the code unbreakable to the enemy.

Though Vardney got all the credit for inventing the device, GTT got all the profits when the patent was bought by the navy. The company argued and produced a release, signed by Vardney before he knew to what section he would be assigned, stating that as the device was invented on company time it rightly belonged to GTT. Vardney never contested the issue but he was warier thereafter.

In the summer of 1936, Vardney went on a vacation to Sweden to visit relatives. It was on this journey that he met a poverty-stricken fellow engineer named Mattias Helmo. Helmo had made a gigantic advance in cipher machines, though at the time no one yet believed his discovery was possible. Accordingly Helmo had been unable to sell his invention and after a series of bankruptcies faced straitened circumstances.

Vardney, still stinging from having been robbed by his employers, immediately did the same to poor Helmo. He offered to buy up the patents for a sum which Helmo leaped at.

Helmo's invention was a pocket-sized cipher machine. Known as the M-210, it became the U.S. Army's medium-level cryptographic system during the war and served in all military units from division to battalion.

Thanks to this fortunate purchase, Vardney could claim a personal fortune topping the million-dollar mark by 1943. Helmo ended up working for the Germans in the famous Pers Z cryptographic section until the day of his arrest for a real or imagined breach of security. Since he never reappeared after the war, it is reasonable to believe Helmo died in a concentration camp.

Though he was soon rich enough never to have to work again, Vardney remained in the employment of GTT. During the war, he was loaned to the U.S. government, becoming a member of the loose group which after the war would constitute the National Security Agency.

All of Vardney's war work was "Top Secret." To mention but one of many devices which he had a hand in developing—the "Huff-duff" or high-frequency directional finder which proved so valuable in winning the war against the U-boats.

When the war ended, Vardney went back to GTT and was soon after named vice-president, Research and Development.

Then early in 1948 he was suddenly fired, apparently following a disagreement over a major change in company policy. However, there was also a rumor that Vardney had become a lush and the company could no longer hide the fact.

With this the record ends.

On the personal side, Vardney married Long Island socialite Elizabeth Ridgeway in May, 1939. The union did not produce children.

Blake threw down the file and swore. Exasperation twitched through his entire body.

What do facts alone tell you about a man's life? Nothing. They don't tell you about a man's demons, about his fears. They don't register the changes that slowly take place, the disappointments, the wear and tear of existence that turns one man into a saint, another into a swine.

Apart from the episode with Helmo, what else did Vardney have on his conscience? Something *was* there,

THE DOUBLE-CROSS CIRCUIT 149

something that one day made him stick a gun into his mouth and blow off the back of his skull.

Blake now knew that UNICOM was some kind of coding machine and that Vardney had probably invented it. But Blake still did not know what UNICOM had to do with Russia nor what Vardney had done since 1948. He did not yet know why Vardney had killed himself. Soon, however, he would. He felt sure of that.

Blake pulled the much thicker file on GTT toward him.

On March 16, 1920, a man breathed his last in Baton Rouge, Louisiana. He was a colorful character, well known in the bayous and on Bourbon Street, part pirate, part *grand seigneur*. He was named Napoleon Wehr, Napoleon because he liked to boast that his grandfather had fought with Napoleon's armies and had it not been for the Purchase he would have grown up a nobleman; Wehr because he liked the sound. And indeed when he was drunk—which was often—he used to roar out his last name like a lion challenging the other jungle creatures.

With Napoleon Wehr's death, his fortune—earned, said his enemies who were many, by war profiteering—passed entirely into the hands of his only son, Nepomucene.

At the time of his father's death, Nepomucene Wehr had just turned twenty-one. He buried his dad, shed a tear or two, and to console himself bought an honorary colonelcy. Then the young Colonel Wehr took all his money and moved to Cuba.

Cuba was delightfully corrupt and made the fleshpots of New Orleans pale by comparison. Colonel Wehr eagerly discovered a vocation as a profligate. But the high life and the mulatto girls soon made extensive inroads into his fortune. It eventually dawned on the young colonel that if he wished to continue whoring in the manner to which he was accustomed he first needed an income.

In 1923, he bought the bankrupt Cubana Telefonica, a small telephone company that had fallen on hard times. Having a somewhatced gradiose view of himself, Colonel Wehr renamed his new company Global Telephone & Telegraph. Then he discovered something about himself he had hitherto ignored: he possessed an instinctive aptitude for business. And what began as mere aptitude soon became genius.

By 1925, the former Cubana Telefonica was turning a profit. In 1926 Wehr began buying other bankrupt telephone companies throughout the Caribbean. Telephones were a new business then and the failures were many, but they did not include Colonel Wehr, who went from one success to another.

The year 1928 saw Global buying heavily in South America. Anything remotely connected to telephones he bought. In Chile he bought into copper. In Argentina Wehr founded a small manufacturing firm. Now he began making his own cables.

In the course of acquiring things, Wehr also discovered how easy it was to buy people. True, he had always suspected this to be the case with regard to women, but he now found that men could be purchased with as little trouble. He began to invest in politicians, in rabble-rousers, in tin-pot dictators—anyone who could help him obtain more telephone companies.

By 1930, Colonel Wehr held either a majority or the largest chunk of shares in eighteen separate national telephone and telegraph companies, not to speak of the companies he owned outright. He had created what the Harvard Business School would one day admiringly call "the Wehr system of selective monopoly."

The following year Wehr opened the New York of-

THE DOUBLE-CROSS CIRCUIT

fices of GTT. While the social pages oohed over the handsome "Latin" millionaire, there were snarky comments on Wall Street made by men who should have known better.

It was during Wehr's stay in New York that an agreement was signed which later came to be known as the Hudson River Exchange. At the time, the main American carriers had not yet discovered themselves to be a natural monopoly, or as the Federal Communications Committee would delicately call it, a "regulated" monopoly. The telephone companies had to compete mightily for subscribers and they greeted with dismay the arrival of newcomers upon the American telephonic market.

The Hudson River Exchange was a document resulting from a meeting of Wehr and representatives of the major carriers. In effect, they said to Wehr: 'What's it worth to you to keep out of the home market?' Wehr named an astronomical sum which was duly paid and the Exchange signed.

The majors made a big mistake that day. For one, it had never been the colonel's intention to tap the home market. For another, they left him with a document which he would later use to blackmail them with threats of conspiracy and price fixing after the majors became "regulated" and learned to live in constant fear of anti-trust actions.

But this was one example of how the Wehr system worked. The young colonel got a lot of mileage out of opening the New York office.

The contribution generously provided by the nervous American competition gave Wehr the wherewithal to begin his European campaign.

To employ a later phrase, Europe at the time was showing its soft underbelly—in particular in Spain where the political situation was beginning to percolate. It was ironic that Wehr, hoping as he put it in his Louisiana drawl "to make a buck out of the Republicans," became instead one of the staunchest supporters of a rebellious general named Francisco Franco.

"*A l'amour comme à la guerre*," say the French. Colonel Wehr might well have added "so too in business." For just as the Spanish civil war became the proving ground for the weapons that were used in the world-wide conflict four years hence, it was also the birthplace of the curious relations involving GTT and the German Reich.

Much given to entertaining on a lavish scale, it was perhaps inevitable that Wehr would meet some of the heroes of the Luftwaffe's elite Condor Legion who by day tested new bombs on Spanish civilians. This happened after Wehr, in return for pouring funds into the Franco war chest, was given an interesting percentage in developing "a truly national" Spanish telephone company.

When he did meet the Condor fliers, they laughingly told him his name meant "war" in German. Apparently the colonel had not known this before and the discovery affected him curiously. He was greatly moved.

Whether this contributed to his subsequent arrival in Berlin is hard to say. It could have, though Wehr rarely did anything without an ulterior motive and mere flattery did not provide a motive sufficiently ulterior.

In Berlin he found to his surprise that the Nazis were snobs. His contacts proved not important enough to get him where he wanted to go: directly to the top. Even a personal letter from Franco did not open all doors.

It was while he sulked in his hotel that Wehr came to know someone who did open all the doors he wanted opened. She was Alexandra Ross, a British aristocrat divorced from an American who was "in airplanes."

Tall, strikingly beautiful in a ghostly way caused by

her dependence on drugs, Alexandra was fascinated by what she called "the greatest social experiment of all time," and that meant what was going on in Germany under Hitler. She had a British decadent's admiration for the Nazis as the embodiment of a Will which the English ruling classes had lost.

Hitler liked her. She personified his dream of an alliance between Britain and Germany and she was often invited to sit at the feet of the Fuehrer while he rambled on following those silent dinners held at the Chancellery.

In short, Alexandra Ross was just the opportunity Wehr needed.

Wehr soon discovered that Alexandra was not exactly what she seemed. In fact, it was after his relationship with her began that nothing involving GTT would ever be quite the same again.

Wehr and GTT obtained the contracts he wanted. Until the United States entered the war, he divided his time between Berlin and New York, campaigning for American's continued isolationism. In effect, GTT became part of the German war machine and remained part of it until the end of the war, a denouement which coincided with Wehr's disillusionment with fascism. And Wehr, who had worked alone until this point, suddenly found he now needed an executive assistant—Alexandra Ross's son, Nicolas.

After the war, Wehr would swear before a congressional committee that GTT had worked for the American war effort all along. After the war, Alexandra Ross—who died of a heroin overdose in 1944—would reappear posthumously as an agent of British Intelligence. And Nicolas Ross, who by war's end had increasingly become the power in GTT while Colonel Wehr increasingly gave himself to drugs and a growing paranoia that would eventually drive him insane, would swear after the war that it was all a vast intelligence operation.

Colonel Wehr told the congressional committee he had become an intelligence operative for the American government back in the South American days. Supposedly GTT provided invaluable services to the Allies in matters of vital importance to the Allied cause throughout the entire course of the war. Supposedly, in the mid-thirties, Wehr was reporting back to Washington details about new German weaponry being tested in Spain.

The fact remains that GTT made fabulous profits supplying both sides with information and material and after the war screamed to be indemnified by the U.S. government for damages caused to its factories by Allied bombing. And the U.S. government paid.

By the end of the war, GTT *was* acting in an unofficial manner for the American government in intelligence matters behind the Iron Curtain.

Backed by its German holdings, GTT in wartime expanded throughout Central Europe. In noneconomic terms, GTT, protected by the Wehrmacht and the SS, bought, in the wake of the Nazi steamroller's eastward drive for *Lebensraum*, cable firms, electrical companies, telephone companies, the usual. Some were bought and paid for, others simply taken over after the Jewish owners had been prophylactically removed.

By the end of the war, GTT still owned substantial holdings in the rear of the Red Army. Increasing numbers of Soviet army commanders found themselves scratching their heads. Here were all these representatives of the German company GTT—there was no doubt in the Russian mind, at least not at this level—who should have been put against a wall and shot. Instead these capitalist hyenas were demanding payments for equipment stolen by the Russians or damages caused by Russian artillery to GTT property!

Even more bewildering were the orders from Moscow that urged the Soviet military authorities to go easy with GTT and either pay up or stall but on no account to act harshly.

For the USSR was bled white by its war effort and was suffering terrible manpower shortages, not to mention capital goods shortages. It needed technology, equipment, technicians; it needed to keep the foreign-owned factories from disappearing to the West, leaving behind empty buildings.

And Nicolas Ross, who to all intents and purposes was running GTT, saw markets, endless Soviet markets that extended almost forever.

What followed in the immediate postwar years was later distorted on the American side to keep up with the cold war line, and on the Russian side in the last wild paroxysms of Stalin's madness and death.

It was not long after that a resounding wave of trials had torn through the Communist camp, putting to the test the elasticity of the faith of true believers. Rajk in Hungary, Paukus in Bulgaria, and the Slansky gang in Czechoslovakia—all devoted Communists since the early days, all accused of espionage for the secret services of the West.

In Russia, Stalin, his brain eaten away by Alvarez's disease, had not yet hatched the dreaded Doctors' Plot in which top Kremlin physicians—most of them Jews—would stand accused of trying to poison the Father of the Peoples.

But the climate for treachery was already ripe and in order to whip the masses into a frenzied hunt for spies, the People's Commissariat of Justice served up a trial in Moscow that came to be known as "the unmasking of the Prokovsky gang of wreckers."

The trial took place early in 1951 and perhaps because the masses had grown too accustomed to seeing wreckers brought to justice during the great purges of the thirties, it was not a huge popular success. But the trial was nonetheless not without interest.

Four men were charged; none of them Russian. All had at some point in the past been employed by GTT. The indictment contained a long list of crimes, the gist of which was that the four, working under the cover of GTT, had actually been employed by British, French, and American intelligence to wreak havoc in the countries of Eastern Europe.

Either the prosecution did a poor job of preparing its case or the intention was deliberate, but it soon became clear as the trial proceeded that it was not the four men but GTT itself that stood in the dock. Not for the usual monstrous reasons expected from "this tentacular bloodsucker of oligopoly capitalism." Instead, GTT was accused of not having lived up to its part in some mysterious bargain, in having "broken the faith erroneously displayed by the proletariat."

This came out in a garbled form. The People's Prosecutor's ravings became even more difficult to follow when he tried to spell out the specific nature of the acts of wrecking undertaken by the accused. Apparently they tried to sell "a death-dealing machine" to the innocent workers. This machine was later referred to as the Sigma machine, though it was never made clear what sort it really was.

The trial aroused the curiosity of Western newsmen, eager to find evidence that the Soviets possessed a death machine more powerful than the H-bomb.

In Washington, the head of the CIA, cornered by reporters for whom the Sigma machine of the trial had turned into the new Russian secret weapon, did something unusual. He launched into an impassioned defense of GTT in the name of free enterprise. Only one crusty left-wing reporter, whom no one listened to anyway, would point out later that it was a curious stand to take. After all, GTT was being tried in Russia, not in the United States.

Back in Moscow, sentence was handed down and predictably all four men were condemned to death by firing squad. Three were shot but the fourth lived—his life spared as a result of top-level intervention by Nicolas Ross. He was Tomas Herscu, later exchanged in Berlin for a Russian spy held by the Americans, one of the first such trades that never came to the attention of the American public.

But it was not until well into the Algerian war of independence that the SDECE showed any deep interest in the affairs of GTT.

The real issue in Algeria was oil. Behind the ragged bands of terrorists who called themselves the Army of National Liberation were far-sighted economic interests for whom it was of great importance that the control of the hydrocarbon deposits in the Sahara be wrested from the French.

GTT was among these economic groups and keeping the ALN and the FLN, the rebels' political front, well supplied with money and guns was very high on the consortium's list of priorities.

In order to dissuade the suppliers of the FLN, the SDECE unleased a spectacular campaign in Western Europe in which terror, assassinations, and bombs were prominent. As a result, the flow of money and weapons to Algeria was reduced to a trickle—but it was never completely halted.

According to SDECE analysts, GTT—operating under a cover corporation—continued to maintain sound relations with the FLN long after the SDECE had supposedly scared it off. When the war ended, GTT was rewarded for its loyalty with the exclusive contract on a custom-made telecommunications system for independent Algeria's national petroleum company, SONATRACH.

As to the identity of GTT's cover corporation, the SDECE never learned. All the threats in the world could not convince authorities in Liechtenstein to allow the SDECE a peek at the records of companies registered in the tiny principality.

Further, SDECE analysts suspected that GTT, in return for services performed, received an oil royalty from the Algerian government. Had GTT managed to become the broker for the major oil companies and thereby assured continued American domination of oil supplies throughout the entire Arab world? If this were so, it could only have happened because GTT benefited from particular consideration from the executive branch of the U.S. government, including the intelligence community.

The file on GTT ended with a breakdown of its phenomenal *percée* throughout Africa and the Persian Gulf in the sixties and Southeast Asia in the early seventies. Like a shadow, GTT's presence seemed to follow the course of trouble around the globe, buying up the ruins of civil war, strife, and disorder. If, in the early twenties, Nepomucene Wehr's act of naming a bankrupt company "Global" had been a gesture of megalomania, by the mid-seventies it had become a frightening reality.

Blake slowly shoved the stack of printouts away to the side of the table, He felt awe-struck and fearful, filled with the kind of loathing and wonder one experienced before monstrousness.

GTT was a leviathan. GTT was a modern-day corporate plague.

THE DOUBLE-CROSS CIRCUIT 159

Blake rubbed his red-rimmed, stinging eyes until they watered. He glanced at his watch. It was after three in the morning.

He lit a cigarette and tried to think.

There was the missing cover corporation where Vardney had to have gone after 1948. In 1951, GTT or—as was more likely—this cover corporation had tried to sell something called a Sigma machine to the Russians. Vardney was a specialist in coding devices. That was what the Sigma must have been, but something had gone wrong. Over twenty years later, would the same thing be tried again? Blake was certain now that UNICOM was another kind of enciphering-deciphering device.

Assuming it was, was GTT or the cover corporation acting for itself, for the Americans, or even for the Soviets? Whom did GTT serve?

Had Vardney belatedly come to understand the truth about the leviathan he helped create? Was that why he had killed himself, leaving just enough signs for someone like Blake—providing someone like Blake were able to read them?

Blake was almost there. He was close enough to intellectually grasp the reasons for Vardney's suicide. But the human dimension, the emotional essence that propelled a man to self-murder, still eluded him.

One man could give Blake all that remained. Nicolas Ross.

"Cerbère!" Blake shouted. "Wake up!"

Several moments later, Cerbère appeared, his face puffy from sleep.

"I need one more thing, old man, and that'll be the end. Subject: Nicolas Ashton Ross, born London, 1911, engineering graduate, Heidelberg, 1931. Nationality: Anglo-American."

A sudden astonishment showed on Blake's face as he said this.

"On second thought, I won't need anything more, *vieux*. It's over. Go home to your wife. Have pleasant dreams."

Cerbére stared at Blake, puzzled.

"You're through?"

"Just about."

Cerbère smiled like a schoolboy let out early from class.

He had removed his white lab coat, shut down his beloved computers, and was at the door when he suddenly stopped.

"Blake, what will happen to you?" he asked almost shyly.

Blake waved his hand.

"Don't give it another thought; I'm fine."

Cerbère nodded, unconvinced.

"All right. Take care of yourself."

"Sure."

Blake returned to the desk and having located some blank printout sheets began to write his report to Santerre. When he was through, he placed the report on the pile of material related to Vardney and GTT. On another sheet, he scrawled a note.

> Cerbère.
> When you get in tomorrow, give all this to the colonel.
> Give it to him personally.
>
> With all my thanks,
> B.

Blake had dismissed Cerbère for one simple reason. He knew where to find Nicolas Ross.

He had not been able to understand why the red dot of Varennes's directional-finder had crossed the Channel to the UK. Not it was clear. Because Ai Quoc, Walter

THE DOUBLE-CROSS CIRCUIT

Price, and the CIA had been working for Ross. And Ross wanted Vardney returned. In the end, the false Vardney did lead Blake to where he needed to go.

To England. Or rather to London. To Nicolas Ross.

It was freezing cold and raining as Blake left SDECE headquarters and began walking down the deserted boulevard Mortier. The wind turned the fine drizzle into stabbing needles of ice.

Blake walked hunched over, listening to the wind howl around him like a restless ghost.

Sixteen

FROM HIS office in the Kremlin, Matvei Gvashvili stared at the lights of nighttime Moscow. He could see orange lights in the apartment blocks, yellow lights still on in the government buildings, and, above them all, the electrified red stars that in Russia replace the neons of the West.

Gvashvili felt disconsolate.

Apart from the weather—it had begun to snow lightly—there was no reason for him to feel this way. Objectively, to cull a word much favored in the language of the Party, nothing was wrong.

Negotiations with the CONSERV team were proceeding apace without obstacles. On the Russian side, the contract eventually to be signed by both parties was almost completed. Even Comrade Leonid Ilyich himself had expressed satisfaction with the technological benefits the contract would bring to the USSR.

So why was this contentment not shared by Gvashvili also?

It was a difficult question to answer since it was based almost entirely on Gvashvili's instinct, on what the Party disapprovingly called "subjective impressions." Not the sort of thing you wanted to put down on paper in case someone later produced your thoughts as proof of "subjectivism"—the philosophical term generally used to explain away a mistake and its perpetrator.

Gvashvili sighed heavily. If only he had something more tangible to go on. But he did not and that was the problem.

Tomas Herscu's behavior was exemplary. He acted exactly as one would expect him to. And Gvashvili did not like that. It was too deliberate—as thought Herscu were waiting for something. But what?

Gvashvili left the window and returned to his desk. Scattered across the polished wood was a mass of agent reports. Whatever KGB agents could be spared from their regular duties had been instructed by their controllers to keep an eye on the main European factories of GTT. Some were able to get jobs in the various plants. Their orders were to report anything, no matter how vague, picked up from other workers that could possibly be connected to the shipments eventually destined for Russia.

Nothing of any value had been reported. Things were too quiet, too normal.

Perhaps Gvashvili would have felt different had he not been involved with GTT in the past—in 1950, prior to the "Prokovsky gang" trial of the following year.

As World War II drew to a close, German military intelligence personnel could clearly read the writing on the wall in letters of fire. They knew that for them the future looked bleak. Death at the hands of the Russians was a certainty. With the Americans it was harder to tell. Many leading American spokesmen at the time advocated a scorched-earth policy toward the defeated Germany: a total dismantling of German industry and the conversion of Germany into a sort of feudal pastureland.

However, there was no unanimity as to how the vanquished were to be treated. One man on the losing side did believe in American magnanimity. He was General Reinhard Gehlen, head of the Foreign Armies East section of military intelligence.

Gehlen was no fool. He knew he stood a far better chance with the Americans to begin with, and that chance could be drastically increased if he came bearing gifts. It so happened that Foreign Armies East was excellently informed on the situation in Russia, on the weakened state of Russian industrial capacity, on Soviet troop composition, and similar information that could prove valuable to the West.

Gehlen's offer was accepted. Most of German military intelligence was absorbed lock, stock, and barrel by the Allies. Gehlen himself went on to become the head of Free Germany's new intelligence apparatus, eventually retiring after a distinguished career.

When the Russians came to take possession of German intelligence archives, rightly theirs, they thought, according to the law of the spoils of war, the cupboards were already quite bare.

In fact, the victorious Soviets, somewhat flushed in that they had almost single-handedly defeated Hitler's armies, were a little put out at getting such a negligible amount of the war booty. To put it mildly, they felt betrayed by their erstwhile Allies. The low-grade intelligence they did get and their subsequent inability to

THE DOUBLE-CROSS CIRCUIT 165

clearly read the intentions of the other side went a long way to making the Russians paranoid.

The situation did not begin to change until after the 1948 coup in Czechoslovakia. Before that, relations between East and West over Germany had worsened steadily. After 1948, they would reach the point of no return. However, when Czechoslovakia toppled rather clumsily into the Communist camp, the Russians thought that at last they were beginning to get what was long overdue them.

In part, it had to do with the advanced state of Czech industrialization which compensated Russia for having lost the lion's share of German industry it wanted.

More significant, as far as Matvei Gvashvili was concerned, was the fact that with Czechoslovakia now Communist, the State had acquired the huge GTT plants in Pilsen.

The two GTT factories were the largest manufacturers of electronic and communications equipment in Eastern Europe. During the war, with a little help drawn from the ranks of the slave laborers, the plants were in the forefront of German high technology in communications research.

The manager of the plants was a Czech named Vaclav Prokovsky, one of the four accused in the 1951 trial; another among them—Tomas Herscu.

The MVD, as the KGB was then known, was most eager to have a long talk with Prokovsky. Gvashvili was picked to obtain Prokovsky's cooperation.

The Czech proved extremely reasonable. With minimal pressure he offered to tell all he knew about the nature of German wartime research in communications and new developments since.

He had a lot to say about an impenetrable code machine known as Sigma. The MVD, starving for hard information since the end of the war, was all ears.

In effect, Prokovsky was "turned around."

Prokovsky agreed. He said he was empowered by GTT's executive vice-president Nicolas Ross to offer not only his services but those of GTT-Czechoslovakia management as well. He said the company wished to collaborate fully with "our socialist friends."

The MVD group under Gvashvili was taken aback. This hardly jibed with their image of capitalist bloodsuckers of the working class. What was the catch?

There *was* a condition, of course; the GTT plants would not be nationalized. The motions would be gone through but instead of the Czech state taking over, the plants would be bought by another firm, CONSERV, S.A.

It was puzzling offer. The Russians were unaccustomed to corporate horse trading. They argued among themselves, Gvashvili going on record as totally opposed to any form of deal.

Prokovsky upped the ante. With the collaboration of GTT in the rest of the world, the Russians would have access to the very latest technological breakthroughs. In exchange, CONSERV wanted to expand into Russia proper.

The issue went all the way to the top, with Beria taking up the matter in a private meeting with Stalin at his *dacha* outside Moscow.

The bargain was struck. Because of his negative attitude, Gvashvili was removed. However, his career did not suffer. Events intervened and suddenly Gvashvili found himself in the unbeatable position of having been right all along—the best posture available for Soviet bureaucratic infighting.

It all blew up over the famous Sigma machine.

Once delivered, the Sigma was taken to a top-secret *sharashka* or research lab where prisoner scientists provided by the MVD labored on the highest priorities of the very government that had emprisoned them. In the words of one of the Stalin Prize winners who took the Sigma apart: "It's intricate and hard to detect but it has been deliberately sabotaged."

Official wrath was swift and brutal. GTT-Czechoslovakia was nationalized in a trice and the plant's entire management arrested.

Abruptly reinstated. Gvashvili was put in charge of the investigation and preparations for the trial.

Gvashvili did not meet Tomas Herscu in person at that time. He was present, observing through a one-way mirror, during one of Herscu's interrogations in the Lubyanka. Herscu showed incredible courage. Gvashvili did meet Nicolas Ross, who flew to Moscow in an attempt to salvage something of the fiasco. But by then it was too late. The Russians took a dim view of being taken for fools and vengeance would be exemplary.

Gvashvili already had few illusions left as to his own capacity for ruthlessness. He was very impressed with Ross's.

At that meeting, Ross made little effort to save anyone's skin but Herscu's. Gvashvili had never been able to figure out why, apart from the fact that Herscu was only twenty-three at the time.

What struck Gvashvili most about Ross was the extent to which his perceptions were unpolitical. Ross told Gvashvili the Russians were making a serious error. He had not known about the defects in the Sigma machine. Without admitting as much, Ross said there had been a mistake. But he was confident an entente could still be worked out.

Gvashvili replied no. He pointed out Ross had exposed himself to arrest just by coming to Moscow. At which Ross had smiled.

Ross was completely, supremely convinced that the day would come when the Soviet State would have to treat with GTT-CONSERV as one equal to another. It was, Gvashvili had felt, as though Ross represented a sovereign state and not a company. It was more than arrogance, it was almost a vision.

Ross was prepared to write off the loss of GTT-Czechoslovakia. What had happened yesterday did not seem to interest him; he lived only for tomorrow.

"There will be a day, Gvashvili, when you will need us," Ross had said, "and you'll never admit it but you'll thank God that we exist."

It had taken over twenty years for that day to arrive, but, just as Ross once predicted, it had.

Russia had never overcome the built-in irrationalities of its industrialization. As chairman of the SCST, Gvashvili was very well informed about the primitiveness of Soviet society as compared with the West. Consistently, Russia lagged behind in the area it could least afford: high technology.

And they were admitting as much when they sat down to negotiate with the CONSERV team.

At times, Gvashvili compared his own country to the China that once thought itself the center of the universe. Forced in the end to trade with the West, Imperial China had let in the very powers that would destroy it.

Gvashvili, as he sat at the negotiating table, saw himself as the Chinese emperor must have once when he first gazed at the blue-eyed barbarians so intent on doing business, so confident in the superiority of their machine society.

He remembered once having seen a top-secret memorandum which Vladimir Ilyich had addressed to Grigori Chicherin, the commissar for foreign affairs, in 1921.

"The capitalists," Lenin had written, "will supply us with the materials and technology which we lack and will restore our military industry which we need for our future victorious attacks upon our suppliers. In other words, they will work hard in order to prepare their own suicides."

Such a vain wish! But what tremendous confidence Lenin showed in the future of the Revolution, in the ability of Russia to overcome her weakness.

If only Lenin had lived longer, he would have found how much harsher the reality was.

If GTT-CONSERV were let into Russia, it would be the West that had triumphed.

Sixty years after the October Revolution, the USSR, entrenched in its own contradictions, unable to advance or retreat without throwing out of balance the hybrid workers' paradise-police state society it had created, would be conceding the bankruptcy of the Dream.

And Gvashvili, in spite of everything, still believed in the Dream—but he knew now that it needed protecting.

Gvashvili lumbered around his office like an aging animal that feels the threat of extinction. He knew the reasons for his unhappiness were not reasons he could share with anyone. He knew he could not break off negotiations for the reasons he wanted to. There was too much pressure on him from above, too many interests already corrupted by lucrative joint ventures with the huge Western corporations.

He needed a reason Russians could understand. A police reason. And he did not have one.

Gvashvili sat down at the desk and stared at his large hands. Once, they had been proudly hard and callused from work. Now they were the soft white hands of a mandarin.

Gvashvili angrily swept the agent reports onto the floor. Grabbing the gold fountain pen from its stand, he scrawled out an order. Go over Tomas Herscu's room once again. No delicacy this time. Tear it apart. Rip out the floors and the walls. But don't come back unless you find some proof they are really here to spy on us.

Seventeen

SEEN FROM the Zaventem autoroute that runs past, the headquarters of the North Atlantic Treaty Organization at Evère in Belgium appears surprisingly like an automobile assembly plant.

It is a huge rectangular complex of buildings with a wide apron of parking lot in front. As the administrative and organizational center of the Western world's largest military and economic alliance, one would expect it to seem more menacing than it does.

At least, such is the impression left with the casual visitor. To a great extent, it derives from the fact that the visitor really does not see anything at all.

Merely looking at NATO HQ, the visitor has no idea of the strict security conditions that prevail within. He is not aware of the rigid compartmentalization that keeps employees in one section totally ignorant of what goes on in the section next door. The visitor cannot see the chambers sunken below ground where military personnel, working in the subdued blue light of the consoles before them, track the deployment of Soviet might on land, sea, and in the air.

In fact, the visitor cannot even see the smaller buildings clustered near the principal blocks nor wonder why these are surrounded by high electrified fences and guarded by soldiers in battle dress, 7.62-mm NATO FN FAL rifles at the ready.

At best—had he been present on the right day and at the right time—the visitor might have seen the arrival of a fleet of Ford vans, painted a metallic silver color with the name CONSERV, S.A. written in dark blue on the doors. And even then the visitor would not have found these trucks in any way remarkable.

The main electronic switching center through which passed all NATO communications was housed in one of these smaller, guarded buildings. Through this center were relayed teletype and telephone communications linking NATO headquarters with the fifteen capitals of the alliance. It was also equipped to handle microwave transmission, boosting the signals to the ground terminal stations scattered throughout NATO territory and interconnected by two SKYNET-type satellites.

Until the CONSERV crews began working on the system, this primary switching center was backed up by a secondary system operating in the United Kingdom. But CONSERV had rebuilt the secondary system right here in Evère; because of the time factor, it had been decided not to lay additional FibrOpt cables—it was simpler to have the alternative system here.

The backup was housed beside the main center. For the time being thick cables dangled from one building to the next. These were the old copper-wire cables that would be dismantled once the new system was "cut over."

The FibrOpt cables, weighing only 1 percent of the copper equivalent, were already underground.

Inside both switching centers, the CONSERV crews were hard at work, among tangles of cable sprouting from the concrete floors. The protective covers had been removed from the switching system, exposing bank after bank of miniaturized circuitry set in removable plastic trays for convenient access. With great skill and delicate gesture, blue-overalled CONSERV employees were wiring and soldering tiny connections.

CONSERV technicians pored over plans covered with the intricate maze of circuit alignments. Others checked off lists of figures that appeared on the screens of the portable testers that verified the circuitry.

Nearby, a representative of NATO's Security Committee watched. From time to time, his walkie-talkie crackled as he spoke with his counterpart on the site of the UNICOM installation.

For the UNICOM was not here but inside one of the principal blocks, specifically within the area known as P Wing—P being the standard bureaucratic designation for maximum security.

The UNICOM was inside P Wing, three floors underground, next to the Situation Center, NATO's War Room, the nerve center of the alliance where the military sorcerer's apprentices practice the science of "crisis management."

In a specially designed room where atmospheric conditions are kept constant so as not to damage the sensitive equipment, where the walls are insulated against any form of interference from microwave bombardment, where the floors sit on springs to absorb the shock waves of a ground-zero hit, stood the UNICOM.

Eric Vardney's brainchild. The most sophisticated coding system ever invented. Total end-to-end encryption, by which the entire process of encipherment, transmission, and decipherment is electronically accomplished—without human intervention. A single all-purpose cipher, simple enough for the lowest echelons, secure enough for the highest, sufficiently variable to provide against interception, impossible to decode if captured. The ideal made real by the genius of one man.

But for now silent. As in the switching centers, UNICOM's three computers were opened and exposed, while a small army of CONSERV technicians checked and made adjustments. Here too sprouted cables from the switching systems, their ends like newly grown roots not yet planted.

Supervised by NATO security personnel, the CONSERV crews labored carefully, with each minute operation bringing the UNICOM closer to the day it would be put into operation.

Until then, however, Vardney's creation, in its gray metal cases proudly stamped in the bottom right corner with the letters GTT, was stillborn.

Eighteen

It was just after 7:15 in the morning when the British Airways-Air Inter shuttle touched down on the runway at Gatwick Airport. The sun glanced off the surrounding fields and cast shadows upon the gently rising hills of Surrey.

In his suit and carrying his attaché case, Blake seemed like all the other businessmen who got off the plane. Since Britain's entry into the Common Market, the representatives of H.M. Customs had showed scant interest in neither Blake or his fellow nationals.

Presently Blake found himself in the main hall. The bright yellow signs over the New Caledonia Airways wickets were harsh upon his eyes.

He walked over to a row of pay telephones. Pulling out the London R-S directory, he flipped rapidly through the pages.

ROSS, Nicolas Ashton . . . 78 Jermyn Street, Piccadilly . . . 01-223-5831. For a moment Blake smiled.

Seeing Ross's name was like catching an oil executive riding to work on a bicycle. No self-respecting telephone executive would think of not being listed in "the book." Or was it that Ross, comfortable in England, home of individual rights, had simply grown careless?

Blake picked up his attaché case and walked down the gangway to the taxi stand outside.

Seated at the kitchen table, Nicolas Ross emptied his coffee cup. He dabbed at his lips with the linen napkin and once again looked at his watch.

What was taking that damn Jenkins so long?

He left the kitchen.

In the antechamber, his suitcase rested near the door, his mackintosh neatly folded over it.

The jacket of Ross's gray suit was in the closet. He took the jacket off the hanger and slipped it on, adjusting his waistcoat afterwards.

Frowning, he walked into the living room. He sat down in the armchair next to the telephone and dialed quickly.

"Yes, this is Nicolas Ross here. I've a nine o'clock flight and my chauffeur has not yet appeared with the car. What is the problem? . . . He radioed he was tangled up in traffic on the Euston Road? Well, why the devil wasn't I told? . . . No, never mind, I'll take a cab."

He had to look up the number.

"Hello. Will you send a car to Jermyn Street, 78? The name is Ross. I'm going to Heathrow. I'd be obliged if you told the drive to hurry up. Thank you."

Ross remained seated in the armchair, his long fingers tapping the sides of his nose. Again he looked at his watch. He'd be in Moscow by noon, London time.

He felt his breast pocket to be certain his passport was there.

Ross heard the sound of a car door slam. Had he been more attentive he would also have heard the engine of an Austin Diesel taxi. None of the taxis one called to be picked up at home were Austin Diesels.

Ross was pulling on his mac when the doorbell rang.

"I'm coming!" he shouted, inwardly swearing at his chauffeur.

The two men stood on the doorstep, staring at each other. The one—the elder, in his mac, his gray hair trim, his eyes enlarged by the lenses of his glasses—startled that the other was not a taxi driver. The other—in his mid-thirties, ready to swing with the attaché case—uncertain whether Ross recognized him or not.

"Mr. Nicolas Ross?" Blake said finally.

"Yes. Who are you? I'm terribly sorry but I've got..."

"I'm Blake," the other interrupted. "Of the SDECE."

Nicolas Ross made a curious throaty sound. Blake lunged, smashing his knee into the older man's groin, then catching Ross as he pitched forward.

"Oi there!"

Blake turned around. The taxi Ross called had drawn up. The driver was leaning out of the open window, concern written across his wrinkled features.

"It's my father," Blake said. "He's feeling a bit faint, that's all. I'm afraid he won't be going anywhere. Sorry for the trouble."

"Shall I call an ambulance?" the driver offered.

"No, he'll be fine as soon as I get him inside."

"Right then, cheerio."

"Thanks, anyway."

Blake dragged Ross back into the house and laid him

down on the carpeted floor. Ross was gasping loudly, clutching at his testicles.

Blake locked the door and drew the chain.

He bent over the prostrate Ross and patted him down for weapons. He withdrew the passport. Flipping it open, he glanced at the visa issued by the USSR Embassy, London, then threw the passport down.

He stood near Ross and waited until the older man's pain ebbed.

"You needn't have hit me," Ross gasped. "I was only surprised. Help me up."

Tensing, Blake did as Ross asked. He assisted Ross into the living room and sat him in the very armchair from which the executive had telephoned for the cab.

Eventually Ross's breathing returned to normal.

"Look, Blake, I've got to be on the nine o'clock Aeroflot flight to Moscow. There's a great deal at stake. Perhaps I can settle your problem on the way to the airport." He paused. "I am fairly wealthy."

Blake shook his head and smiled.

"Your goons thought so too."

"Thought what?"

"That I could be bought. I'm not interested in money, Mr. Ross, I've come here to talk with you."

Ross sat up and looked at his watch. There was not much time left.

"I fail to see how your talking with me will accomplish anything. My position has always been extremely straightforward: I want Vardney back. Why you have chosen to be so obstinate is beyond me."

"My position is also simple, Mr. Ross. I'm trying to understand why Eric Vardney shot himself. I believe only you can tell me the answer."

Ross stared at Blake for a long time. Various expressions went through his features. Especially striking was the look of horror that briefly appeared in Ross's eyes and was then covered over.

"He shot himself? When? How?" From his tone, it was the one possibility he had clearly never considered before.

Keeping his eyes on Ross, Blake snapped open the attaché case. He took out a brown folder and slid it across the carpet.

"A little over three weeks ago, a man was found dead in a low-class hotel in Paris. He was to all appearances derelict—threadbare, worn out. With a service revolver, he had blown off the top of his head. These are the photographs taken in the morgue by the PJ. I believe there's also one from the room where he was found."

Ross took out the photos. Blake thought he saw the older man's hand tremble. Ross looked at the photos one after the other.

It surprised him how moved he felt seeing Vardney dead. Though Vardney in killing himself had cheated Ross of the pleasure. Though Vardney in killing himself had ruined everything.

Ross removed his glasses.

It was all over.

"Well, Blake, Vardney's death does put . . . recent events in Paris in a different light. I know this may sound peculiar but had I known he was dead . . ."

"You know now, Ross," Blake said coldly. "Your remorse, if that's what you're trying to express, does not interest me. I want to know why Vardney killed himself. I want to know now."

"And my plane to Moscow?"

"You won't be on it. You can always take a later flight."

Blake looked at Ross with eyes dry as parched earth.

"Very well, Blake. And as I imagine you are armed, I am aware I have little choice in the matter."

Blake did not reply. Ross stared at him a moment, his face reflecting bewilderment. Suddenly Ross stood up, then immediately sat down again.

"Do you have a cigarette?" he asked nervously.

Blake reached into his jacket and tossed Ross the pack. Ross's hands shook as he lit the cigarette.

"Where shall I begin? I . . . I loved Eric. You see, Eric and I were brothers . . . ."

Not in the blood sense, but joined together by the bonds certain friendships cannot possess, bonds which once tied can somehow never be broken.

They were the same age, though their birth dates were not the same. Physically they resembled each other; both were blond, thin, with long faces. In later years, Ross would flesh out while Vardney would remain gaunt. But that was later.

They met quite by accident, as most significant meetings begin. It was in Stockholm during the long delightful summer of 1936, at the Grand-Hotel Saltsjöbaden, an enchanted waterfront castle. Two young men in their prime—one, recently from Berlin, in Stockholm to clinch a deal with the Swedish telecommunications firm Eriksen; the other on holiday and in his pocket the patent rights recently acquired from the engineer Helmo.

A collision in the lift. Conversation. Both discover each other's American accent. They agree to have a drink at the bar.

If it sounds like the beginning of a love affair, it was. It happened so naturally neither had any inkling it could become something other than a spontaneous celebration. For each, mesmerized by the discovery of an image of himself, it was a somewhat drunken expression of narcissism. Above all, each was free to do as he wished. Only later would the form they had chosen by which to express love reveal the destructiveness it had always contained.

Ross, whether by luck or by design—he never really knew—had for the first time in his life moved out of the domineering shadow of his mother. Nepomucene Wehr had given him what he craved most: his freedom, and it enabled him to discover a greater craving—for power.

Ross was barely beginning to comprehend the power of GTT. He who only months before was still a child now sat down with commodores of industry as equal to equal. Ross had tasted the fruit of power and liked the taste. His mother would have said it was because he had the proper breeding. Whatever the cause, he had come into his own.

And so had Vardney, by a different path. It would be simplistic to say he had discovered that crime does pay. But his coup with Helmo had opened his mind to the possibilities inherent in money. He had begun to admit his dreams to himself and they were not the straight-and-narrow dreams of his parents.

What drew the two together was their ability to treat each other's dreams as real. Had they been older they would have known that dreams, for all their glitter, are dangerous things, but they were only twenty-five and everything was possible.

They talked for hours, mostly boasting, behaving as though their dreams had already come to pass. And in a way they had, or at least they were just beginning to.

Out of it came a pact.

Ross bought into the Helmo patent. It was a fair deal. GTT would market and sell the portable coding machine for a percentage; the major share of the royalties would be divided 60 percent to 40 percent between

Vardney and Ross. Of course, Vardney could have retained 100 percent ownership, but could he have sold it? Ross was offering GTT's connections and GTT's resources.

Vardney always assumed, when the first big order came through, that the U.S. Army was the sole customer for whom GTT produced the M-210. It was not until after the war that he learned the Ober-Kommand Wehrmacht had also had the coding machine.

In the summer of 1936 it was different. Here was success; no one bothered to inquire at what price.

Originally Vardney had wanted to leave GTT. Ross persuaded him to stay on. Over the two of them always planed the shadow of GTT. Ross was very much aware of this; Vardney not. But Ross had understood at least that without GTT he was nothing. Vardney erroneously imagined that he himself was free.

To the shadow of GTT would be added another. Elizabeth Ridgeway, who in May, 1939, became Mrs. Eric Vardney. Outwardly Nicolas Ross was all smiles over the engagement and very much the proud best man at the wedding. Inwardly he felt Eric had broken the pact—there was someone else now who, by virtue of her position, would have to share their secrets and they never were meant to be shared.

To Nicolas, Vardney's marriage was the opening shot of the war. By the time he and Eric came to sort things out it was too late.

Vardney's marriage failed essentially because there were three people in the bed. If Nicolas wasn't actually in the house, he was on the phone, calling from all over the world, indifferent to the hour in Long Island. Nicolas had urgent business to discuss with Eric; nothing could be more important. And Eric was never able to convince Elizabeth of the great truth this represented.

The inevitable eventually happened. In Eric's house. In

THE DOUBLE-CROSS CIRCUIT

Eric's bed. And Eric, trusting fool, had left them alone, "the two most important people in my life."

The onset of the war papered over the cracks in personal lives. All would have to await V-E Day for the strains to finally bring down what had already stood up for too long. By then the destruction of Eric Vardney by Nicolas Ross had burst into the open.

Vardney's attitude to the war was that of a patriotic American. He divested himself of shares in GTT-Germany; or rather left it to Nicolas who simply bought them himself.

Vardney labored for all he was worth for his side to win. Exhausted, overworked, stressed, he began to drink more than he should have. Nicolas would eventually give him several reasons to drink more.

As would only emerge long after World War II, the British and Americans gained much useful information from a high-level coding device known as Ultra, installed, thanks to a Polish spy, in England before the war.

The Germans, for their side, had an equivalent from which they got a fair amount of mileage. The American M-210 courtesy of GTT. Possession of the coding machine almost helped the Germans win the battle of the Ardennes.

This was the information Ross threw in Vardney's face soon after the war. There was a special account in Switzerland carefully kept by Ross which totaled to the last *pfennig* Vardney's contribution to the German war effort.

Ross offered Vardney the money. In the same breath, he announced that Elizabeth was leaving him and filing for divorce. Ross would marry Elizabeth as soon as the divorce came through.

Vardney never recovered. Profoundly wounded both in his professional estimation of himself and in his masculinity, he gave himself to drink with a near-fanatical vengeance.

Ross's marriage to Elizabeth was just a way of turning the knife in the wound. Still, it took her two years to realize Nicolas was only trifling with her to get back at Eric for marrying in the first place. After her second divorce, Elizabeth never remarried. From a distance she watched the strange conflict that possessed her two ex-husbands.

At first Ross had expected Vardney to take revenge. But Eric, tortured by remorse and self-pity, appeared satisfied with the demons of booze. Increasingly Nicolas despised Vardney as a coward, as a worm he liked to toy with but who no longer threatened him.

He entangled Vardney in contracts to CONSERV, contracts which Vardney signed in a drunken haze, indifferent to the clauses. Ross bought Vardney as a property among the others. Absorbed in the growth of CONSERV, he neglected Vardney for long periods though he always made certain the scientist was kept supplied with acohol.

Vardney was a pet, caged, imprisoned.

It was the catstrophe in Russia over the Sigma machine that made Ross understand Eric still had fangs. The discovery pleased him.

The Sigma machine had been yanked out of Vardney piece by piece, Ross taunting the poor scientist, telling him he would now do for the Soviets what he had unwittingly done for the Nazis. By cutting off Vardney's supply of drink, Ross drove him into cooperating against his will.

Vardney avenged himself by sabotaging the Sigma with an inbuilt defect in design.

Flushed by Vardney's show of spirit, Ross revealed to Eric that his stupid gesture had caused the death of three more men. He wanted to confront the horrified Vardney with the wives and children of the three shot in Moscow. He pushed Vardney so hard Vardney slashed his wrists with pieces of a whiskey bottle.

"You will die when I want you to, not before," Ross told Vardney when the scientist regained consciousness only to find himself still alive.

So began the years of Vardney's captivity. One time, after Vardney attempted to escape, Ross smashed his leg and left him chained to the cot of the room at the School in Bletchley Park.

And, all the while, Ross continued to force Vardney to work, knowing that only work kept him sane, stopped him from tottering into the state of madness on whose edge Ross wanted him to stay.

Those were the conditions in which Vardney created the UNICOM, the most sophisticated enciphering system ever designed.

Once again, Vardney outwaited Ross, becoming the pliant creature, submissive, cooperative, sold totally to the Devil.

And then he escaped and, this time, he made it.

Blake realized he was sweating. In part, it was caused by the content of Ross's narration, by the horrific account of the perverse love between Ross and Vardney. But there was more.

It was Ross's tone, so gentle and level as he recounted the atrocities perpetrated against Vardney. There was a nostalgic quality in Ross's voice, a wistfulness almost.

Ross had spoken candidly—at least Blake felt Ross was not trying to deceive him. Yet it was not the candor of honesty; it was the candor of a man in whom there is no trace of a moral scruple.

Ross was silent now, observing the young Frenchman

across the room. Blake's face must have shown something of his feelings for Ross suddenly spoke:

"Come, come, young man, don't look so disapproving. I tried to answer you to the best of my knowledge."

Blake's features were once again frozen and expressionless. Ross smiled unexpectedly, a smile not without charm.

"Now, I'll ask you a question. Why this interest of yours? What was Vardney to you? You never knew him, yet it is very important to you to understand why Vardney no longer wished to live. Why?"

Blake seemed surprised, even though he had repeatedly asked himself the same question. Until the moment he knew the answer.

"I never knew my father," Blake said quietly. "I saw him only once when I was in my teens. It was a disappointing encounter. Because of it I did not think about him again. Until the day, years later, when I received a letter from his wife. In this letter she told me he had killed himself in the garage of their home. With a gun, like Vardney. A mutilating, inexplicable death—like Vardney's.

"She said she did not know why my father had done this. Perhaps I knew. He thought about me often, she said. Since that day I have not ceased to think about him. It tortured me. The last time I had seen him I was needlessly cruel—as only the young can be. What happened to him afterward I never knew. Until he was dead and it was too late for me ever to find out.

"I could not escape the feeling that somehow I had caused his suicide. Had I tried harder to reach him, perhaps it would never have taken place.

"He, my father, looked a bit like Vardney. Fatter . . . but from the minute I saw the file on Vardney, I felt, I knew, I had to understand why this man had killed himself. It was a way of reaching my father." Blake fell silent.

After a moment, Ross nodded.

"I see." It was more an acknowledgment of the fact Blake had spoken than anything else.

"Well, Blake, if I've been able to help you, I'm glad of it. I still have a plane to catch." Ross stood up.

"I'm not finished, Mr. Ross."

Ross looked irritated, then slowly sat down.

"What is it?"

"Saundra Letellier—does the name mean anything to you?"

"No. Should it?"

"Considering you caused her to die, it should. I imagine it was your order given to one Walter Price that led to her death. She was slit open like a fish by a Vietnamese working for the CIA."

"Blake, I give many orders. How they are executed is not my concern. I never ordered the death of this person."

"Nevertheless, I hold you to account for it. So at the very least you can sit back and wait until I have no further questions."

Ross sat back in the armchair. There was an irrational streak in Blake which he had no desire to bring to the surface.

"Very well," he said. "Proceed."

Blake shifted a little in the other armchair. The PA-15's shoulder holster was digging into his chest.

"It has struck me, Mr. Ross, throughout this . . . investigation, that the closer I get to understanding it, the more it slips away from me.

"What you said about Vardney was of considerable help. But I am obliged to go beyond Vardney now. Vardney was the victim. He was only one half of a relationship. You are the other half. Do you see the problem? Now I have to understand *you*, Mr. Ross, and I do not."

And yet the mystery of Ross was no more profound than that of any man or child. He had been caught upon the anvil of his parents and hammered into shape by the circumstances of the times.

A too-demanding father, who had not wanted a child, and could only be impatient with Nicolas's immaturity, John Ross, the engineer, measured performance alone and had no room within for love.

It was the times, also, which took the boy's father from him, as John's dissatisfaction widened until he could no longer stand flaccid Europe, prostrate from the trauma of the Great War.

America, a man's world, beckoned, and there John would find, in the pioneering years of military aviation, the rewards he had not received from his son. There too he would heal himself from the collapse of his marriage to the bored Cambridge beauty who was left to bring up Nicolas alone.

For Alexandra, the years after 1918 were an opiate, a time of frivolity and experimentation in which to lose oneself from the grim memories of the four long years of war.

Nicolas became her plaything, a toy on whom she vented her frustrations, a fellow experimenter in the exercise of freedom to do anything at all.

Nicolas grew up thoroughly degenerate. And bored.

It was boredom largely that made him resume a schooling that had gone the way of all flesh several years before. He returned to the mathematics which had briefly fascinated him in his early youth and studied in secret.

His mother's German phase had resulted from a dabbler's interest with Expressionistic painting. In 1929, she decided to move to Berlin.

Nicolas obtained his engineering degree in 1931. A remarkable feat since he was almost completely self-taught prior to university.

Nicolas at twenty-four was still larval. Something, someone had to bring out what was hidden inside. That person was Colonel Nepomucene Wehr.

Wehr was the only man Ross ever spoke about with an affection not tinged with more violent emotions. As with Vardney, whom Ross genuinely loved, he would destroy Wehr as soon as he got the chance.

Alexandra and her son were the closest Wehr ever came to having a family. For Alexandra, Wehr was another distraction, reminding her perhaps of John Ross. To Nicolas Ross, Wehr was a father in that ideal definition of fatherhood which consists in giving a son the wherewithal by which to make his own way in the world.

Wehr gave Nicolas a sort of love. But, better, he gave him GTT. It became everything, replacing family, friends, any other interests. It was so much greater than he and would be able to keep ahead of him no matter what he did in the future.

In a way, Ross's friendship for Vardney was the last expression of what human feelings remained in Nicolas. After Vardney, he would never again know a normal relationship with another person. Ross became GTT.

"None of this would have come to pass without Colonel Wehr. It was necessary; for GTT to be created, for its particular structures to be established.

"But, you see, Colonel Wehr was still of an age when the last vestiges of political man were vomited forth from the turmoil of the collective unconscious. I was not. It was clear to me, perhaps because I was able to see Hitler and his ilk from close up, that the world could no longer afford the luxury of political views.

"If you look at the history of wartime business, you'll see that many companies kept careful accounts on contracts made before the war—the British armaments industry, for instance, which had patents on German shells. For each shell fired, the Germans owed the British so much. They too kept accounts. It was all settled after the war.

"Businessmen are the only people who have faith in the future of mankind. No one else does.

"After four years of war, did they—political men—learn anything? No, not a thing. They were ready to begin all over again with the Russians.

"Not I. The Russians were there; supposedly Allies. They needed us. I was ready to stake my company on good relations with them. I was not wrong, but political man was still alive.

"You people in intelligence are a prime example. You understand nothing. Your aims are minute and silly. But if I go, as I have done, to the CIA and say 'Look, we want to get into Russia; we'll gather intelligence for you there as long as you don't interfere with us,' suddenly they think it's a wonderful project. What's the difference? They can only grasp what is mean and puny.

"They are all like that—governments. Be it the Americans with their Trading with the Enemy Act, or the Russians with their morbid fear of foreigners, it's all pettiness and terror and those are not receptive climates for business.

"I have been an American spy. It helped me obtain what I wanted. I supported the Nazi war machine and I would gladly work for the Soviet Union if I had the chance, if my own objectives were met as a result.

"That is why GTT is a multinational. It belongs to no

THE DOUBLE-CROSS CIRCUIT 191

country whose narrow political aims would interfere constantly with a much greater, much more important objective.

"Political views are a condition which like a fever must run its course. If the peoples of the earth insist on being fools, that is their affair. We will help them be fools if they want; we will profit from their foolishness; we will use man against himself and one day he will thank us for having saved him.

"In the short span of fifty years, GTT has implanted itself in 70 nations; at any given moment night or day over a half-million employees execute my will; the governments that can harm me are very few and they will be fewer still. Within fifteen years, GTT companies will answer to no one but our board of directors. We will have enough economic might to ruin the majority of countries on this earth and seriously harm the others. We will be listened to very attentively.

"Then you will all see something never seen before. Peace. Not politician's peace, but real peace. Cooperation between the nations. Above all, order.

"For the first time in the history of man, a rational global economic order is at last possible. There will be no more rich and poor nations. The world will consist of one market and it will be divided up into economic units in which everything functions for the greater good.

"In the meantime we will grow upon the turmoil men create. We will feed on civil wars, on strife and bitterness that we are not responsible for but that others bring about, we will devour all that is wrong as a maggot eats the unhealthy part of a wound.

"But one day the wound will be clean and then it can heal on its own.

"GTT is the logical result of all of economic life, Blake, its culmination. The future."

Nineteen

BLAKE STARED at Ross, mesmerized. Ross's long explanation was not the speech of a madman. In a horrifying way it made a kind of sense. It was thought-out, clear and logical, though spoken with a reticence one finds only in the deeply private.

For a moment, Blake saw Ross as a man, tortured by his solitude, abysmally alone on the cold pinnacle from which he viewed the world below, cut off by the distance from all the warmth of life, yet trying to express what he alone could see.

For a moment, Blake felt something of what it must mean to be Nicolas Ross. He could not help but shudder.

It was too high, too remote. Did that explain the inhuman quality in Ross's voice, the nearly metallic sound of the words?

The voice was rational—as a computer with a vocal

unit might sound. Once a man's, it had become the voice of a leviathan.

"All things and people have their place, Blake. For a brief instant, our two worlds interconnected. Because you asked, I have described something of my world. I trust you understand now.

"That was what you wanted, was it not? You said money does not interest you. Very well, then logic must. I have tried to show you why our two worlds must remain separate each from the other. There is no point insisting further. Return to your world, Blake. As I must to mine."

Nicolas Ross looked at his watch.

"I have none to return to, Mr. Ross," Blake said quietly.

"No, Blake, that is not so. All you have to do is walk out the door; your world is out there. It is recognizable. Mine is not, nor can I simply get up and leave."

Blake did not move.

"The truth is, Mr. Ross, that you are a Soviet agent, isn't it? And once you go to Moscow where Vardney's UNICOM is, you won't come back. Why should I allow you to succeed?"

Ross shook his head.

"It was foolish of me to expect you to understand more. No, Blake, I am not a Soviet agent. I am a man who's slowly growing old. Therefore, I will not attempt to wrestle with you to convince you you are mistaken. I *will* ask you this then:

"If I can prove to you I am not, will that satisfy you?"

"Perhaps."

"No, Blake, not perhaps. Yes or no. For your interest, UNICOM is not in Moscow at all, it is at the headquarters of NATO. I'm sure your organization will be able to confirm that. Fair enough?"

"All right."

"Then we will go to the officers of my company. It is only there that I can provide you with ocular proof I have been completely frank with you."

Blake felt himself grow tense at the thought of penetrating the leviathan's lair.

Tomas Herscu was whistling as he stepped out of the elevator. The sour-faced floor clerk mechanically handed him the key to his hotel room.

Herscu bowed to her, a gesture which only made her eyes narrow suspiciously.

He resumed whistling as he walked down the corridor. The burnt-out light bulb had not been replaced.

The negotiations were in their final phase. Much of the daily sessions were now taken up with nit-picking over specific formulations that would appear in the contract. Hardly stuff overwhelming in importance, but satisfying after the long hard haul.

Gvashvili seemed bored and restless. The burly chairman had left early today, after an aide, squeaking across the marble floor in new shoes, had whispered in Gvashvili's ear.

Herscu inserted his key in the lock and turned it. The door swung open with its habitual creak.

The room was a total shambles.

Holes had been made in the walls. There was plaster dust everywhere. The carpet was ripped out and the floorboards underneath pried loose.

Herscu's clothes were scattered throughout the room, sleeves torn out of shoulders, padding ripped open.

His suitcases had all been dismantled, the locks broken, the backs slashed.

THE DOUBLE-CROSS CIRCUIT 195

In the middle of the floor sat the laser telephone, circuitry gutting from the shattered casing.

Matvei Gvashvili was in one of the armchairs. Near him stood a man in a black overcoat.

Herscu was suddenly pulled forward. He tripped on one of the loose floorboards and fell.

Behind him, another man slowly closed the door of the room.

Herscu, his face deathly pale, pushed himself up on his hands. He got to his feet and began dusting off his trousers.

"Excuse my colleague, Mr. Herscu," Gvashvili said jovially, "he's an ill-mannered lout."

Gvashvili's gray eyes sparkled.

"What is the meaning of this, Mr. Chairman?" Herscu asked woodenly, his voice hoarse.

Gvashvili pointed to the smashed laser telephone.

"And that, Mr. Herscu, isn't that proof you are a spy? No, don't answer; we'll know soon enough."

Gvashvili got to his feet.

"By virtue of the Criminal Code, Article 48, you are under arrest on charges of espionage. I have no doubt you will be found guilty, and, in due course, shot. Gentlemen."

Gvashvili, enjoying the role of impresario to the full, turned to the man next to him.

The man pulled a pair of handcuffs from his pocket and advanced toward Herscu.

Herscu was staring at Gvashvili, his eyes wild.

"Why?" he gasped.

There was a rapid series of clicks as the handcuffs were snapped across Herscu's wrists.

"It would take too long to explain here," Gvashvili said, amiably tapping Herscu on the shoulder. "But we'll discuss it soon, my friend." Gvashvili's voice lowered. "In the Lubyanka."

Herscu's eyes wavered, then the whites appeared as he pitched forward in a dead faint.

After the two men had dragged the prostrate Herscu from the room, Matvei Gvashvili remained behind alone. His air of feigned joviality was gone; his features were cold and set.

His eyes raked the room.

"*Sobaka*," he murmured to himself, "you were lucky this time."

Like a great many Marxists, his only justification resided in a blind faith in history. The history of the future.

As though it were suddenly freezing in the room, Gvashvili shivered.

In his office at the SDECE headquarters, Colonel Edgar Santerre finished reading Blake's report.

He was angry. At himself, at the director of the SDECE, and at Blake.

At himself because he had agreed to go along with the director's suggestion that Blake be the sacrificial victim just so the SDECE would be absolved of responsibility in the "goings-on" of the last few weeks. On Santerre's desk was the report he had written for the director to present at the afternoon Cabinet meeting. This report made a plausible case for Blake's "mental illness." In writing it, Santerre had rationalized that it was better for Blake to be kicked out of the SDECE as mentally unfit and the matter forgotten than for him to be turned over to the PJ on charges of murdering Ai Quoc.

Santerre was angry with the SDECE director for being such a goddamned bureaucrat. And in the best bureaucratic tradition, worrying only about whether he was covered in the hierarchy. Santerre's report had admirably covered for the SDECE. It was all the American's fault and Blake's. The minister of the interior would be more than satisfied.

Santerre tore up the report he had labored on so carefully.

He would write another one, and he would enjoy the thought of the SDECE director recommending Blake for the Légion d'honneur.

But Santerre's decision did not change the fact that he was furious with Blake. He got up from his desk and walked over to the window. Somewhere out there was Blake.

"You crazy fool," Santerre murmured, "why did you risk it alone?"

The taxi pulled up before Centre Place. The building's height created a wind tunnel on the ground below. The water from the stainless-steel fountain lashed in a needle-fine spray.

Blake got out after Ross. Red double-decker buses rumbled across St. Giles' Circus, the stink of poor-quality diesel fuel hovering in their wake.

Ross was walking toward a concrete gangway that led into Centre Place. The wind tore at his hair and made his mackintosh crackle. Following him, Blake was hit in the face by the spray from the fountain. Momentarily blinded, he began to run. But Ross continued to walk ahead; he was not trying to get away.

The wind was a high-pitched scream as the two approached the main entrance.

Ross produced a key and unlocked the metal-and-glass doors.

In the lobby, it was strangely silent after the artificial gale outside. Blake's ears were still ringing.

A guard sat behind a console, watching an array of TV screens.

"Hello, Mr. Ross," the guard said, grinning obsequiously.

Ross replied with a nod. Blake noted the holster on the guard's hip—most unusual for England where the police are unarmed except for special assignments.

Blake was acutely aware he had passed through the invisible frontier and was now in the land of GTT. Inside the leviathan's lair.

As the brushed metal doors of the express elevator closed behind him, Ross pressed the button for the eighteenth floor. Blake saw a light go on on the panel above. CONSERV, S.A., the panel read. The cover corporation.

Blake stood a little behind Ross. His hands were sweating. He undid his jacket button and, reaching inside, released the safety on the PA-15.

... 16 ... 17 ... 18.

The doors opened with a hiss.

Blake saw a wood-paneled lobby with the letters CONSERV, S.A. in silver on the wall. Slightly to the left, near three plush leather chairs, was a desk. Behind it sat a man of Blake's age, wearing a cream-colored suit.

For a second the man looked puzzled and Blake knew instantly he was Ross's bodyguard.

"Harris!" Ross shouted as he broke into a run. "Get him!"

Harris's arm snaked toward his heart.

Blake dropped to his knee.

It all seemed to happen in slow-motion.

Ross's head was a gray blur. Harris's arm was stretching toward Blake, the automatic's blind eye trying to find its target.

Blake fired twice, then flattened himself onto his stomach.

THE DOUBLE-CROSS CIRCUIT

He saw Harris throw back his head and twist to the left. In Harris's neck a hole suddenly opened, a gush of blood sprayed like a geyser. Another hole appeared in Harris's shoulder. Blood squirted across the cream-colored suit like ink on a blotter. Harris slowly tumbled backward. There was no sound as he fell onto the thick carpet.

"Ross—don't move!" Blake yelled, moving his arm in the direction of the executive. Ross froze.

Blake waited. He heard gurgling issue from Harris's throat. Then there was silence.

"Any more surprises?" Blake called out. "You're dead if I hear anything."

"He was the only one," Ross answered.

Blake stood up.

He walked behind the desk and looked down at the dead Harris.

"That was stupid, Mr. Ross."

Ross gazed at Blake.

"You're beginning to annoy me," he said, and for the first time there was emotion in his voice.

"Who else is on this floor?" Blake asked.

"No one. Only my offices. That was my secretary."

"Is that the only elevator?"

"To this floor, yes."

"How can I keep it here?"

"Harris has a key that will lock it on this floor."

"Any other doors or entrances?"

"One on either side of the lobby. They have locks; Harris has the keys."

"Where is your office?"

"There—on the right."

"Open the door. I want to see inside."

Blake pointed the -15 to Ross's head.
"Do as I say, Mr. Ross."

They were in Ross's office now. Blake quickly took in the teak paneling on the walls, the gracefully arched ceiling, the long conference table, and the panoramic view of London.

Ross walked over to one of the walls and slid back a panel. Blake saw a bank of electronic equipment.

"That's the receiving unit for a laser telephone," Ross explained. "My director in Moscow has the transmitter. It enables us to communicate without the knowledge of the Russians."

Ross moved toward the desk. Blake shifted his position so he could see Ross's movements.

Ross pulled open a drawer. Blake's finger tightened on the trigger of the -15.

Ross lifted out a folder and handed it to Blake. Keeping his eye on the executive, Blake flipped open the cover. He glanced down and saw correspondence, the eagle-topped crest of the CIA, and the printed letters "Office of the Director."

"What's this?" Blake asked, looking up.

"Communications between myself and the CIA director. GTT is nominally an American corporation; for reasons of national security it is forbidden to trade with the Russians on the scale I propose. But CONSERV is not subject to American law and can, yet CONSERV is not GTT and does not have GTT's resources.

"For GTT to be involved, I needed the permission of the American government. As I said to you earlier, they will approve what we do if we reduce it to their level.

"Therefore I proposed that we, once established in the USSR, supply them with information. They could not refuse. We are the first Western communications firm to

THE DOUBLE-CROSS CIRCUIT

have access to the Russian market as extensively as we will.

"On the other hand, it was only normal for the Russians to suspect us of trying to spy for the Americans. We had to convince them this was not so.

"We had created UNICOM for NATO. What better gift to bring to the Russians than the new communications brain of the West's foremost military alliance?

"That was our reserve bargaining counter. The Russians know we're light-years ahead of them in the field of high-technology communications. The fact we were ready to offer them systems they just don't have the capacity to develop themselves would, we felt, be sufficient reason for them to sign with us.

"But the Russians are a suspicious people and, judging by their past record, quite capable of rejecting our offer. We needed an argument convincing enough on its intrinsic merits to guarantee the successful outcome of our negotiations. UNICOM was that argument.

"Yet these things work both ways. As a result of our signing a major contract with the Russians, we did not want the Americans to think we had double-crossed *them*.

"That was why, before the Russians got UNICOM, we were going to modify the system so as to restrict Soviet access to NATO communications to certain but not all channels—and this would be done with the agreement and the foreknowledge of the Americans. Modifying the NATO UNICOM was to be a 'black propaganda' operation, a top-level exercise in disinformation.

"This was what Vardney was working on when he took flight. To his befuddled mind, I was only repeating the Sigma incident, I was selling out to the Russians. He could never accept that, this time, the U.S. government was a willing party.

"It's all in the folder. Does it make sense to you now,

Blake? The reason I wanted Vardney back was that we have a deadline to meet for the NATO UNICOM. He had to finish modifying the UNICOM circuitry so the Russians could access.

"Now that he's dead, the deadline cannot be met. That is why I am going to Moscow: to gain time while we try to finish modifying UNICOM. Is it clear?"

Standing behind the desk, Ross glared angrily at Blake.

"Quite clear, Mr. Ross. Except for one thing: five people have died. Explain that."

"That is your level of it, Blake, not mine," Ross replied steadily.

Behind Ross, Blake could see the toylike cars and trucks moving through the London streets. People the size of ants.

" 'That is your level, Blake, not mine,' " Blake repeated.

The telephone console on Ross's desk began to beep. Ross hesitated.

"Answer it," Blake said. "Business as usual, Ross." His tone was bitter.

Ross picked up the receiver.

"Yes? . . . Hendersley, I can hear you." Hendersley was the number-two man on the negotiating team in Moscow.

Ross did not say another word for several long minutes.

Blake saw Ross's face turn white.

When he spoke again, his voice was low and constricted.

"Will they allow you to leave? . . . Be on the next plane then. . . . No, there's nothing more we can do. Goodbye."

Blake saw Ross grow old before him. The executive seemed to shrivel, to become a dried-out husk that stared blankly at Blake through foggy gray eyes.

But Ross's voice stayed surprisingly calm.

"You can make that six dead, Blake. Tomas Herscu's been arrested; they'll shoot him now. It's finished. Had I gone there when I was supposed to, it would have ended differently."

He continued to stare at Blake.

"There will be no contract with Russia. There will be no work for the people who would have gained employment as a result. The Russian market was almost without limit—steady, guaranteed growth without strikes, without labor problems, without recessions. It would have broken the circle we are caught in here. We are still the prisoners of capitalism's ebb and flow, with its unemployment, with its depressions.

"What are six people next to the thousands who would have gained? How many more will die now because they won't find work?

"Long ago, Blake, long ago, I learned there's no such thing as morality. You are like Vardney in that respect; you believe in good and evil. And when you think you are doing good, you only make things worse."

Ross's eyes appeared to focus. Now he looked at Blake as though he were seeing him for the first time.

"You *are* like Vardney! You are his strong side; you have the blind stupid courage he did not. Now I know why you are here. You are Vardney's revenge and you have come to kill me.

"The avenging force of the meek, that is you. Not content with what you have already destroyed, you must go all the way. Destroy the monster and soothe the conscience. You are defeated but you can still kill. In your outrage, you protest the fact that you have lost.

"Go ahead, Blake, carry out Eric Vardney's vengeance. Like all men, none of you can bear to look the future in the face and say, 'Yes, that is what we have created.' I did and it did not frighten me. Do not think I am frightened of you now. I *am* the future, Blake, and you will live to see that I am right!"

Blake heard the metallic voice and it seemed to resound within his brain, an echo endlessly repeating.

He raised his arm, extending it outward. Ross's eyes bore into his.

Blake squeezed the trigger.

Behind Ross, the floor-to-ceiling window exploded outward. There was a rush of air inside the room; papers flew like birds suddenly taking off.

The wind howled, tearing at their clothes, sucking at them both. Blake dug his heels into the carpet.

Ross, pulled back by the force of the expelled air, had lost his balance. His hands tore at empty space; a shriek came from his throat.

He clutched at the wildly flapping curtain. His face was contorted with the effort of trying to save himself. Drowned by the scream of the wind, the curtain tore as though without a sound.

Blake saw Ross's eyes bulge out as Ross tipped backward into emptiness. He seemed to hang suspended in midair, arms and legs flailing, then suddenly he dropped and began the plunge to eternity, eighteen floors below.

Blake stood on Westminster Bridge, leaning against the railing. Below him, the gray-brown waters of the Thames moved sluggishly toward the sea. Behind him, on the left, the delicate crenelations of the Houses of Parliament were outlined by the afternoon sun. To his right, on the south bank, stood the imposing beige structure of London County Hall.

He was staring at the water, almost longingly. As though he were contemplating whether or not to throw himself over the rail.

He had thought of it, then thought better.

It was done. As Ross had said, he could still walk out into his world.

Blake raised his head. The next bridge crossing the Thames was Charing Cross. Further ahead, Tower Bridge. On the left, St. Paul's.

He looked toward the Embankment, his eyes searching for the gilded eagle whose beak pointed directly toward France. He could not see it.

It was done. He felt exhausted, sad and calm simultaneously.

Regretful? Yes, deeply. Not for the way it had ended, but for the fact it had begun. And yet he felt like Lazarus risen from the dead and was grateful for being resurrected.

He straightened up. Reaching inside his jacket, he unsnapped the empty shoulder holster and pulled it from him. He folded it and dropped it over the rail.

Blake heard the hoslter splash as it hit the water.

Again he reached into his jacket.

His *carte d'identité* went next. Then his *livret militaire*. His *carte d'électeur*. His passport was last.

He watched his identity float down the river, then turned and, with his hands in his pockets, began walking toward the Parliament buildings.

He was free.

What would he become? He did not know. Nor did he care. He had a little money. It would be enough for now.

Where would he go? He did not know. For now all he wanted to do was walk.

Later he would visit his father's wife. He still needed to know what kind of man his father had been.

The package was brought to Colonel Santerre as he

was reading the newspapers. He immediately recognized the handwriting.

Santerre tore off the paper and found himself holding a packet of letters stamped with the emblem of the Central Intelligence Agency. Correspondence between the CIA director and Nicolas Ross.

Santerre's eyes moved to the screaming headlines of the afternoon's editions.

TOP EXECUTIVE'S SUICIDE ROCKS LONDON BUSINESS CIRCLES

The newspapers were having a field day. The president of the huge GTT empire, apparently involved in a homosexual relationship with his secretary, kills him, then throws himself from his skyscraper office.

Santerre looked back at the CIA letters. In the brown paper of the package, he found a note.

It read:

> Colonel,
> The enclosed correspondence between N.A. Ross and the director CIA will fill in whatever gaps there were in my last report. I will not be returning to France. Do not try to find out where I have gone.
>
> Adieu.

Twenty

NATO's NEW UNICOM system was cut into operation just in time for the December Annual Military Review.

At this top-secret meeting, the fifteen nations of the alliance get together to map out their hardware requirements for the forthcoming year. New weapons systems are examined upon the recommendations of the military chiefs-of-staff. Decisions are taken as to what systems to develop, what contracts to allocate to what firms for the building of sophisticated new weaponry.

At this meeting, all the information is highly classified for the obvious reason that it contains the military future of the alliance.

It has long been the dream of Soviet Intelligence to obtain some of the information exchanged at the Military Review. Only Matvei Gvashvili would know how close that dream was to coming true. But he had chosen to disregard this dream in order to save another, that of keeping Russia pure.

The new UNICOM was shown to the privileged Nuclear Group countries' representatives at the end of the Military Review. Everyone was impressed and agreed that GTT had surpassed itself.

And of course it had. The UNICOM contract was the only one GTT-CONSERV ever honored to the letter.

When the UNICOM became operational, it was exactly what Eric Vardney had designed it to be.

In the end, Tomas Herscu was not shot as a spy. Soviet methods are no longer what they used to be. Instead, he was incarcerated in the psychiatric hospital at Sychevka. Here, according to the testimony of recently exiled dissidents, the prisoners are subjected to regular, heavy doses of the drug *sulphazin* whose therapeutic powers include reducing a man to the state of a vegetable.

The embarrassment produced by the death of Nicolas Ross eventually subsided. Soon after, the board of directors of GTT was able to appoint a suitable replacement.

The new president is a man greatly liked within the organization. He commands respect and loyalty.

But, more important, the board is confident he will soon bring GTT stock back up above the $70 per share mark which it held unwaveringly toward the end of the Ross years.

CONSERV underwent a major reorganization. Its center of operations was moved out of London to an unspecified location.

CONSERV is still in business—under a different name today.

Not long ago, someone close to the company was overheard to boast:

"If we were ever investigated, Watergate would be a gnat in comparison."

ABOUT THE AUTHOR

Michael Dorland is a Canadian journalist who also taught modern history at two leading Canadian universities. He formed the ideas for the novel while working for a large multinational corporation. He lives in Montreal, Canada, with his wife and child and has just completed his second novel.

Recommended Reading from SIGNET

- ☐ **THE STAND by Stephen King.** (#E9013—$2.95)
- ☐ **NIGHT SHIFT by Stephen King.** (#E8510—$2.50)
- ☐ **CARRIE by Stephen King.** (#J7280—$1.95)
- ☐ **'SALEM'S LOT by Stephen King.** (#E9000—$2.50)
- ☐ **THE SHINING by Stephen King.** (#E7872—$2.50)
- ☐ **SAVAGE RANSOM by David Lippincott.** (#E8749—$2.50)
- ☐ **THE BLOOD OF OCTOBER by David Lippincott.** (#J7785—$1.95)
- ☐ **VOICE OF ARMAGEDDON by David Lippincott.** (#E6949—$1.75)
- ☐ **CITY OF WHISPERING STONE by George Chesbro.** (#J8812—$2.25)
- ☐ **SHADOW OF A BROKEN MAN by George Chesbro.** (#J8114—$2.25)
- ☐ **SUNSET by Christopher Nicole.** (#E8948—$2.50)
- ☐ **BLACK DAWN by Christopher Nicole.** (#E8342—$2.50)
- ☐ **CARIBEE by Christopher Nicole.** (#J7945—$1.95)
- ☐ **THE DEVIL'S OWN by Christopher Nicole.** (#J7256—$1.95)
- ☐ **MISTRESS OF DARKNESS by Christopher Nicole.** (#J7782—$1.95)

Buy them at your local bookstore or use coupon on next page for ordering.

SIGNET Books You'll Enjoy

- ☐ BEDFORD ROW by Claire Rayner. (#E8819—$2.50)†
- ☐ SWEETWATER SAGA by Roxanne Dent. (#E8850—$2.25)*
- ☐ FURY'S SUN, PASSION'S MOON by Gimone Hall. (#E8748—$2.50)*
- ☐ RAPTURE'S MISTRESS by Gimone Hall. (#E8422—$2.25)*
- ☐ THE LONG WALK by Richard Bachman. (#J8754—$1.95)*
- ☐ DAYLIGHT MOON by Thomas Carney. (#J8755—$1.95)*
- ☐ MAKING IT by Bryn Chandler. (#E8756—$2.25)*
- ☐ THE CORAL KILL by Bryn Chandler. (#E8347—$1.75)*
- ☐ ON THE ROAD by Jack Kerouac. (#E8973—$2.50)
- ☐ THE DHARMA BUMS by Jack Kerouac. (#J9138—$1.95)
- ☐ FLICKERS by Phillip Rock. (#E8839—$2.25)*
- ☐ MADAM TUDOR by Constance Gluyas. (#J8953—$1.95)*
- ☐ THE HOUSE ON TWYFORD STREET by Constance Gluyas. (#E8924—$2.25)*
- ☐ FLAME OF THE SOUTH by Constance Gluyas. (#E8648—$2.50)
- ☐ ROGUE'S MISTRESS by Constance Gluyas. (#E8339—$2.25)

* Price slightly higher in Canada
† Not available in Canada

Buy them at your local bookstore or use this convenient coupon for ordering.

THE NEW AMERICAN LIBRARY, INC.,
P.O. Box 999, Bergenfield, New Jersey 07621

Please send me the SIGNET BOOKS I have checked above. I am enclosing
$_____ (please add 50¢ to this order to cover postage and handling).
Send check or money order—no cash or C.O.D.'s. Prices and numbers are
subject to change without notice.

Name _____

Address _____

City_____ State _____ Zip Code_____
Allow 4-6 weeks for delivery.
This offer is subject to withdrawal without notice.